Elusive Treasures

Elusive Treasures

Hy Ron & Juaneta

Good thing Arvilla didn't know all this, or she would have run all the way home ~

Dell R. Fo

9/29/2014

Dell R. Foutz

Library of Congress Control Number:		2014914229
ISBN:	Hardcover	978-1-4990-5809-3
	Softcover	978-1-4990-5810-9
	eBook	978-1-4990-5808-6

Rev. date: 08/19/2014

To order additional copies of this book, contact:
Xlibris LLC
1-888-795-4274
www.Xlibris.com
Orders@Xlibris.com
622983

CONTENTS

The author holds a fine gold nugget from the gold fields in Siberia, USSR, in 1989. Our Russian guide demanded that I give it back to him after the photo was taken.

Gold recovered from a mercury retort at a placer gold operation at Dewey Bridge, Utah. The owners said it was from "a few days" effort with a sluice box and a front-end loader.

INTRODUCTION

When I started to write this book, I was advised by wise friends not to tell the stories in the first person. However, much of the book is autobiographical, and I felt compelled to write it in first person. I hope it is not a disaster. The various episodes in the book range from absolutely true from start to finish, to a few that start with a real incident but wander off into fiction. One story is entire fantasy.

A Little about the Author

I was born in 1932 in the old Dee Hospital at Twenty-Fourth and Harrison in Ogden, Utah. Everyone knows that was a bad year in the U.S.; and shortly after I was born, they tore down that hospital and built a much bigger one a few miles away. Possibly, they moved the hospital because I was born there, but I never figured out the connection. Later, when I went to Weber College and they moved the school while I was trying to finish a two-year degree, I began to wonder if something about me created some kind of jinx for things. My folks thought they had enough children when I was the third child, but even that went haywire twelve years later when a pair of twin girls came into the home. It was a good family with five of us kids, and they encouraged me to do well in school.

I think my dad gave me an allowance, but it wasn't much because he always provided the real necessities—like fishing equipment and hunting gear. Santa Claus helped, too, with BB guns and a bow and some arrows. It was a good life coming out of the Depression with enough money for my dad to teach me the essentials for providing for a family. I learned how to safely handle a gun and how to swim. What else mattered if you planned to survive on ducks and pheasants, deer, rabbits, fish, and a few vegetables you could grow in the backyard? We always had a couple of peach trees too, an early variety and a later one. Everything was planned nicely. Dad was a dentist and could afford to provide some of the best fishing in Utah, Wyoming, Idaho, and Montana. It was great for me and my older brother. I think my three sisters had a little child neglect from a father that was a man's man.

Treasure Number 1

A PROPER EDUCATION

In second grade, I got into trouble with Mrs. Hegler. She was a tough gal I got crosswise with, and she could take only so much of my behavior. She called my folks to tell them I was misbehaving, and I was glad she called my folks because my dad would tell her a thing or two. On the scheduled day, I waited around until after four p.m. when Dad could get off work and take care of Mrs. Hegler.

"Hello, Dr. Foutz, so glad that you could come," she said.

"What seems to be the trouble?" he answered.

"I am having a little problem with your son."

"For instance . . .?" Dad asked.

She cited about three things that would indicate that young Dell was a genuine pain in the neck—or other parts of the anatomy. In each instance, my dad looked at me and asked if I had done what she had told him. In each case, I started to rationalize my actions by saying something like "Well, er . . . uh yes, but . . ." And in each case, my dad would stop me when I got to "but" and ask for more instances. To each one I admitted "Yes, but . . ." That was good enough for my dad. Our meeting was over very quickly once my dad really told her a thing or two. It was something like: "Do whatever it takes to make him mind, and if it doesn't work, tell me about it."

I knew that my dad had once been the sparring partner for the all-army heavyweight boxing champ in Chicago while he was in dental school at Northwestern University. I got the message, and by the time school was out for my second grade, I was the spelling champ in my class. If my father had not intervened in my "education" that year, I might have been among the youngest school drop-outs for the entire state. I found out that learning can be fun, and after some tough years, at the age of thirty-four, I ended up with both US Air Force and US Army pilot wings, a PhD in geology, and five kids.

TREASURE NUMBER 2

MARBLES

At about age ten, I played a lot of marbles and got pretty good. We always played "keeps" and not "funsies." In keeps, the winner keeps what he wins each game. I was good enough to win bags of marbles in our neighborhood. But a kid that lived down the street turned out to be a little better, and soon he had all my marbles. Thinking I could win them back if I just had a few more marbles, I went to my dad's office and conned him into giving me a quarter to get some Jergen's hand lotion for my mom. I took the quarter to the variety store and bought a nice bag of marbles and—wouldn't you know—that neighbor "friend" won them all before the day was over. When I got home after being cleaned out of all my marbles, my dad had already talked with Mom about the hand lotion. The next hour was as good as a long sentence in a juvenile correctional facility. Dad did not spank me on this occasion, but he and my mom used a great moment to teach me a lot about honesty. It must have worked because later in life, my wife laughed at me once in a ghost town in Nevada when I would not park in the most logical place because there was an old sign painted on the wall of a long-abandoned building that said: "No Parking." She teased me often about that one. Perhaps the second most important lesson I got then was that I would not win my fortune playing marbles in some international marble championship. My only consolation was that Gary Jesperson, the neighbor kid that cleaned me out of my marbles, became runner-up in the Utah State Marble Championship. How could I ever achieve greatness if I had lost my marbles before I was twelve?

Treasure Number 3

GOLF BALLS

Even in the 1940s, a good Titleist or Spalding
Dot golf ball was worth about a dollar.

Dad was a good golfer, and my earliest money was made at the local course where I shagged balls for him. This was in the days before driving ranges. He would hit a bag of balls at me, and I would avoid getting hit and retrieve all the balls. I was quick and had good eyesight, so he was not really trying to hurt me. I do remember being spanked a couple of times; but twice was enough, as I learned to mind my parents. The golf course gave me a chance to find things of value with a little effort. As a ten-year-old, I had much delight in finding lost golf balls. Errant balls would turn up in strange places, and I never tired of tramping through the toughest brush to find them. I think something in my genes makes me search for hidden treasure. At first on the golf course, I was too small to caddy. But my father was a personal friend of the golf pro at the El Monte course; and for a kid, I made good money selling golf balls to the pro. I was not very old when I made my first $20 in only one week. There was a strong rule that we were not to approach the players to sell them golf balls. Even back in the 1940s, a new Titleist golf ball or a Spalding Dot was worth a dollar, as I remember, and depending on how many "smiles" it had, a used ball might be worth 75 cents. A smile was a curved cut in the white cover caused by a dubbed hit, like when the golfer looks up too quickly and hits only the top of the ball. Modern balls don't get smiles. My favorite players were the ones that could really whack the ball, but would give it a little spin to make it curve to the right (a slice) or the left (a hook) and send the ball into my hunting grounds.

I have found balls in tree crotches more than eight feet above the ground and in rodent holes. Most places where I have played also had rattlesnakes, so the rodent holes were not checked very thoroughly. In those early days, most golf balls were made with hundreds of feet of elastic rubber string wrapped into a ball with a tough cover. Rubber strings were a lot of fun, especially in a bonfire when a golf ball would be pretty entertaining as it would twitch and flip around as the strings burned. Modern balls are not so entertaining. And try as I might, I cannot put a smile in the new covers even with my worst hits.

One of the holes on the old El Monte course had a small stream that ran through some heavy rough then cut across a fairway, making a nasty hazard. If a player made a nice long drive toward the green, the ball would reach the little stream, and the current was usually strong enough to take a ball into a horrible thicket on its way to the nearby river. Right at the downstream edge of the fairway, where the stream hits the thicket, there was a hole where a ball might drop out of the current and stop. One day when the water was a bit low and clearer than usual, I could see a ball in the hole. I reached in, and to my surprise, I found eleven balls in there. A delightful "treasure" for a kid my age. Some of them were badly weathered and not even white, suggesting that they had been there a long time, perhaps years. I checked the hole often after that and usually found more treasures. One time, the treasure was an angry crayfish, so I learned to search cautiously.

I learned to play golf too, and when I was about fifteen, I was playing alone in the early morning at the El Monte course when I came to the tee of hole number four. It was a short par-three hole with a straight level shot at a small green. A man was on that green ahead of me, and when he saw me waiting on the tee, he waved me on to hit my drive before he finished putting his ball into the hole. I was small for my age and pretty unimpressive for any kind of athletic competition, but I put my ball on a tee and gave it a mighty whack with a number 3 wood. The ball was cleanly hit, and with a little fade to the right, it stopped about twelve feet short of the pin. The man waited for me to get to the green, and as I approached, he commented on what a nice drive I had made. I was pretty nervous to have an audience, but I stepped up to my ball and casually tapped it in the hole for a birdie 2. Again the man complimented me for a nice birdie. I tried to be casual, as if I always played that well, but I didn't tell him that it was the first birdie I had ever made, and I was about as excited as a boy could be. He allowed me to finish the round with him, and I played fairly well for the rest of the round, but not nearly so well as that first birdie hole.

I could shoot in the '80s in high school. I tried out for the Ogden High School golf team and also entered a caddy tournament, but I found that the pressure of playing for something other than just pleasure was a little unnerving for me, and I played poorly in any kind of competition. My fortune would not be made as a professional golfer. Besides, Ben Hogan (the winner of the US Open in 1950) only won $4,000. Anyway, when I finished high school in June of that year, North Korea jumped into my plans by invading South Korea.

Much later, as a professional geologist, I often thought of my "golf-ball sluice box" while checking corrugated pipe on a gold-bearing stream. I have, in fact, found a few "colors" of gold in corrugated pipes under culverts. I checked a culvert near the top of Red Mountain Pass in

Colorado's San Juan Mountains and found no gold. But, at that site near the head of the Uncompahgre River, I didn't find any gold in the stream either, even though there are a number of gold mines within very few miles of the culvert. Near Leadville, Colorado, in the campground west of Twin Lakes, there is a stream that carries a few flakes in the gravel, and I did find a little gold in the riffles of a pipe under a bridge. Where the Ogden River, in Utah, exits the Wasatch Mountains and spreads out a little in the valley, I have panned a little gold just downstream from the highway bridge at the old Riverside Gardens. In fact, in the Great Depression of the 1930s, I hear there was a man working in a pit for a sluice box at that very site, and he was killed when the pit collapsed and trapped him. It is the same old adage: "Gold is where you find it." As a longtime gold addict, I have learned some of its secrets and have an edge on where to look for it and how to recover it. But I digress. Golf balls have little to do with valuable treasures in gold.

Treasure Number 4

URANIUM, OF COURSE

A geologist graduating in Utah in the 1950s would have to have some experience with uranium. My father was a dentist, but he was always dabbling in something else. He and some of his bowling buddies in Ogden, Utah, had made an automatic pin-setting machine that was installed on a single lane that they had built in a machine shop. It worked pretty well and was in the testing phase when I lost track of the development. I saw it in operation once, and I was impressed because I had done some pin-setting work while working my way through college. In fact, about 1952, I was a pin-setter at Provo, Utah, the night the bowling alley caught fire, and I remember pushing all the rental balls out of the racks and trying to roll them outside to save them before the ceiling caught fire and we had to evacuate the building. I remember the incident quite well because the girl I eventually married was bowling that night while on a date with another guy.

I do not know what happened to the automatic pin-setter, but I remember my father explained that Brunswick soon came out with a pin-setter that had some components that were remarkably similar to parts of their design. I think they challenged Brunswick about their design, but Brunswick is a big company with lots of lawyers, and nothing came of the challenge. Dad also made portable duck blinds and goose down socks for really cold duck hunting—both years ahead of advertisements for them in *Outdoor Life* magazine. He patented an over-the-counter remedy that would help all kinds of ailments, especially those encountered in his dental practice. He liked prospecting, and he filed claims on mica deposits and especially uranium prospects in Nevada, Utah, and Wyoming.

One day before I had graduated from high school, my father called my brother and me to a little experiment in the stock market. He wanted to explain to us what a boom market was. My brother was born in 1928 and I was born in 1932. I am not sure when we did the experiment, but the uranium boom of the late 1940s and 1950s was under way. I think Charlie Steen had already made his huge discoveries near Moab, Utah. My dad was following the penny stocks of uranium companies, and he explained that there was a "uranium boom" going on, and a lot of money would be made in the penny stocks. He said that for a while, many companies would go after uranium, and some of them would find some uranium and others would go broke. He suggested that we each invest an imaginary $10,000 in the penny stocks and see if we could make some imaginary money. We each picked a $10,000 portfolio from the published penny stocks that were listed in our daily newspaper. He had been following the news in the market and was much more knowledgeable than my brother or me. In six months, we checked our results. We all made significant profit. Dad's increase was much more than ours, but the concept of a boom market made a lot of sense after our little experiment. The few companies that became successful made a big jump in the market, while some of the others went broke. In the six months we followed the trends, the losers didn't lose much because the stock was so cheap, and the good companies more than made up for the losses.

In the 1950s, the Atomic Energy Commission (AEC) made some aerial surveys with very sensitive radiation detectors and published maps that would show the radioactive anomalies. One Friday, we got a copy of a brand-new anomaly map for an area in Wyoming where my father had prospected earlier. There was a strong anomaly in an area we were familiar with, and we wanted to be among the first to check it out on the ground. We loaded up some Geiger counters and headed for Wyoming in the middle of the night. I was riding in the backseat, and a little before daylight on Saturday, they told me to get our equipment ready because we were approaching the location of the strongest radiation anomaly. When I switched on the first Geiger counter, it indicated that we were already in the anomalous area. We stopped the car, and in the early light, we realized that it was a pretty strong anomaly. Instantly, I had gold fever—only this time it was uranium fever, and I had it bad. My heartbeat increased, and in a few seconds, I imagined what I would do with the millions of dollars my family was about to make. A new house and new cars for each of us, and mine would be a new Jeep station wagon and a Piper Tri-Pacer airplane to go along with it. And I would travel to Alaska and New Zealand. According to the AEC map, we were still several miles from the best area. We drove a little closer to the proper place, and the Geiger counters continued to give high readings. After circling around a bit, we finally realized that the whole state of Wyoming appeared to be in a radiation anomaly, and we were in the fallout area of a nuclear test in the Nevada Test Site.

Nuclear tests near Las Vegas were big in the news while I was attending college in Provo, Utah. On one occasion, the newspaper listed the day and time of one of the above-ground shots. As a student, I had a four a.m. to seven a.m. janitor job (it was called "custodial services" in those days), and I was assigned to the Heber J. Grant Library with several other students. We emptied the trash, swept, mopped, waxed some of the floors, and tidied up the restrooms. On the day of the nuclear test, the detonation was planned for 6:55 a.m. Our janitor time ended at 7 a.m. We decided to climb out on the roof of the library to watch. We had a portable radio that was carrying the story on the test shot, and we looked to the south as the radio gave the countdown. It was still dark, so it must have been in the winter, and the road distance to Las Vegas is about 375 miles. The test site is north and west of Las Vegas but still a long way from Provo, Utah. As the radio gave the countdown and he called out "zero," there was an impressive white glow on the horizon. The size of the glow was much larger than a basketball at arm's length in front of my face. I excitedly climbed down from the roof and clocked out of the building and rode my bicycle the mile or so from campus to my home on Fourth North Avenue. When I got inside and began explaining the incident to my wife, the dishes and windows began to rattle as the shock wave arrived. I had witnessed the explosion of an atomic bomb!

In the south part of the Shirley Basin in Wyoming, my dad and his brothers found some interesting radioactivity at a place called Black Buttes. Their Geiger counters gave some very promising readings along the face of a gently dipping outcrop of sedimentary rock. Digging into the outcrop with rock picks, they gathered some yellow-stained material that was definitely "hot." Assay samples were taken, and claims were staked. The assays came back remarkably high with several percent uranium. The only trouble was that the samples had been taken of the yellow stuff that had been scraped off the cracks in the bedrock. They had high-graded the deposit. Assays of the whole rock would not have been so impressive.

I had a break in my college classes, so I joined them at Black Buttes. We discussed the situation, and I and others agreed that we needed to see if the "hot" stuff got better as the rocks dipped away from the outcrop—or if the outcrop was just a small isolated trace of uranium. We decided that our best approach should be to get a drill rig on the location and drill a few holes away from the cliff face and see if the deposit got better at depth. All indications were that it should get better as we got deeper and farther away from the weathered outcrop. It was an exciting time for me, although I was just a kid in school. It was, however, graduate school; and it was in geology. Uranium fever did not overtake me.

That particular month, my uncle Duane (who was selling Kirby vacuums in Montana at the time) was the only brother that had time to spend on the location. He had a serious case of uranium fever. He was unable to find a driller to work on the location quickly, so he hired a dozer to come in and scrape away the face of the outcrop and get into the ore that he knew was just a little deeper. The next time the rest of us could check on the location, Duane had bulldozed away most of the money that was available to develop the prospect, and the "ore" deposit had been scraped away. There was no rich lode deeper and farther away from the surface outcrop. I saw some of the yellow coatings, and they turned out to be high-grade autunite, a complex uranium phosphate.

This little episode at Black Buttes was not far from some incredible deposits of uranium farther north in the Shirley Basin. The irony is that when other companies made their huge discoveries in the Shirley Basin, they used the discovery date of my dad's claim to get the big bonus money from the AEC for discovering a large deposit of uranium in the basin. By the time the big producers came on the scene, the bonus years had expired, but my dad's claim was early enough to qualify for the bonus. But Dad's claim did not lead to a significant discovery. I understand that my dad and his brothers tried to get some compensation from the big companies, but again, the companies had a lot of lawyers. My best opportunity to get a real fortune in the uranium boom was gone.

"Boom markets" returned to me while I worked for Exxon in Corpus Christi, Texas. Our offices were in the Wilson Building, and there was an office for Merrill-Lynch on the ground floor, right next to the sandwich shop. Some of my Exxon pals would spend part of their lunch break watching the stock prices on the big board on their way to and from the sandwich shop. One fellow in particular said that offshore oil exploration was in a classic "boom." He had invested in companies that built offshore drilling equipment. Things like crew boats to take workers to the rigs and specialized helicopters that would be needed for shuttling the drilling crews out to the rigs. Even underwater welding stuff. Anything that would be used in offshore drilling and production. He said one time that he was making more money on the stock market than his salary at Exxon. I was hearing really good advice, but failed to act on it.

TREASURE NUMBER 5

CHICKEN BOUILLON

"Gold is where you find it" is an old adage, but sometimes the stuff shows up in very strange places. For my last few months as a pilot in the USAF in 1959, I was stationed at McClellan Air Force Base, near Sacramento, California. I was about halfway through the transition training to fly the C-121 Constellation when my superiors found out that I was going to be discharged before I could be certified to fly the "Connie." They cancelled my flight training and assigned me to be the weather briefing officer for the crews that were flying around the clock in the early-warning radar "picket flights" about 200 miles off the US West Coast. I could still log my flight hours in the C-121 with my radar crew, but I would not be first pilot on any of the flights.

"Four in the afternoon and no wind! Sure, we can make it—Hah!"

Doug Oglesby—at age twenty-four a ruddy, towhead blond with a crew cut—was a very young-looking captain, and he grimaced as he told me our takeoff time. We would try to take off with a full load of people, fuel, and six and a half tons of radar on a short runway. It would be "iffy" with a twenty-knot headwind; but in dead air, there was not much chance.

McClellan was having its main runway extended just for days like this, and we now had to use an alternate shorter one while the best runway was under repair. Our weather briefing said that the high today would be about 104 degrees, and that would hit about four p.m.

"Hey, Doug," I called, "look at the bright side. Hartshorn is sick today. That ought to be worth 500 feet of runway." (Hartshorn is a huge radar observer of about 270 pounds.)

"That's a start." He scowled through his nearly transparent white eyebrows. "Too bad you can't toss out a couple of those consoles."

Doug was referring to the heavy, refrigerator-sized radar consoles in the "back" of the plane. Doug's job was to fly the plane, but I was in charge of all the "stuff in the back," as he always referred to it. In the "back" were twelve men and six big radar consoles with a huge plastic operations map. We had a pair of talented young corporals behind the map that wrote all the information backward with a grease pencil that glowed in the darkened "operations room." Our plane was the four-engine RC-121D, one of the first early-warning "AWAC" planes in the air force. I was the radar director, but Sergeant Chavez and his crew knew more about the radar than I did. I think they put officers in charge so that they could blame someone with rank when something went wrong.

It was 1959, and our briefing mentioned some solar flares a couple of days running that would mess up radio transmissions. It was the IGY of all things. IGY stands for the "International Geophysical Year" when the eleven-year cycle of sunspots would be the most intense since scientists had been monitoring them. Radio communication had been marginal all summer, but today would be worse.

The hot afternoon was dragging, and we delayed going out to the ramp as long as possible so that we could stay in the air-conditioned ready room. A little after three p.m., Doug got up and said, "I'm afraid it is time!"

Doug and the copilot, Lieutenant Izer, led us out; and the navigator, flight engineer, my twelve-man radar crew, and myself straggled behind in a sloppy single file. We had our chutes and flotation gear plus a variety of junk. Captain Oglesby had a flight case stuffed with information to fly anywhere along the Pacific Coast. Weather was often a problem, and we never knew when fog would close McClellan. Many of our other choices often got fog too, but this day should have been okay.

Doug and Izer did the walk-around inspection, and I got my crew settled in "the back." I told Sergeant Chavez that I would watch the take-off and then come back when we got over the water. Today's flight would be to San Francisco and straight out about 200 miles due west from the Faralon Islands. We would orbit at 10,000 feet all night and be home before lunch (the next day)—maybe.

The C-121 is a sleek long-range, four-engine plane with a triple tail. Its main distinction is very long, very skinny wings for long-distance travel. President Eisenhower once had one as Air Force One. The reconnaissance version, the R model, has an ugly round radar dome under the midsection and a big fat dorsal fin for the height-finding radar antenna. The nickname "pregnant guppy" is very appropriate. Long three-bladed propellers on a low wing forced the plane's landing gear to be tall. It was the tall stance on the ground that made the plane a natural choice to carry a radar dome under the belly.

Engine number 4 was just spluttering into life when I entered the cabin.

"Can I have the jump seat for the take-off?" I asked.

"Sure—*if* we take off." Doug was still worried about the high temperature and no wind on a short runway.

When the engines were all chugging smoothly at idle power and the air-conditioning was starting to have some cooling effect, Doug signaled for chocks out. The brakes released, and the big plane inched forward. After about five feet, Doug made a quick stop for a brake check, and then the plane began to creak and wallow forward. He cranked the little wheel by his left knee to turn the steerable nosewheel, and we headed for the active runway, which was a couple of miles away.

Doug stopped short of the active runway and headed partly into what little wind there was and watched the gauges as the flight engineer ran up each engine to nearly full power, checking the magnetos on each and looking at an array of gauges to make sure everything was "sanitary."

"We're good," he said.

Doug began to straighten the heading back toward the active runway, and immediately, the tower called us with "6288, you're cleared for take-off."

Izer clicked his mike and said "6288."

We crept onto the runway. Doug used a sweeping turn to get as close to the end of the runway as possible then lined up with the centerline and came to a complete stop. Flaps were set, and all four engines slowly revved up to maximum power until the plane was nervously shaking and roaring as Doug stood hard on the brakes.

"Here goes nothing," he yelled as the plane eased forward.

Izer was to watch the airspeed and check at the "go-no go" marker on the runway to see if we had 98 knots. At 80 knots, Izer shouted, "Eighty!"

The big plane lurched along, rattling, rumbling, and shaking. I looked out at the left wing, and the big tip tank was bouncing up and down as if we were flapping the wings for take-off. Doug squeezed the control column with white left knuckles and gritted his teeth to try to get another horsepower or two out of the throttles with the white knuckles of his right hand.

"We only have ninety!" Izer screamed over the roar of the plane as we passed the "go-no go" marker.

Doug chopped the throttles and got back on the brakes. He jammed a little, jammed again, and more. Finally, we stopped on the edge of the gravel overrun for the runway. Cranking the little nosewheel gear and giving power to the right outboard engine, Doug brought the big bird around, and we went back to the first exit and headed down the taxiway back to the other end of the runway.

"Without some wind, we'll never make it," Doug muttered disgustedly.

We loped along the taxiways and back to the run-up area. Izer soon called the tower to say, "This is 6288 ready for take-off, maybe!"

"Hold short, 6288, we have one on final."

"6288 holding short."

The incoming RC-121, with its belly dome, seemed to hover like a whale just above the concrete then touched down gently almost in front of us. The main gear screeched and smoked, and the plane rolled ahead several seconds before the dual nosewheels finally made their puff of smoke.

As the plane began its exit turn, we heard "6288, cleared for take-off."

"Roger, 6288."

Again, the sweeping turn, full power, shaking and roaring, and we surged forward. Near the "go-no go" marker, the gauges were shaking so much that the airspeed needle was swinging all the way from 85 to 110 knots.

"Maybe ninety-five," Izer yelled.

Doug looked at his right hand on the throttles, and then just pushed harder and harder. We were committed.

The nosewheel came off the ground, but the main gear continued to roll. The plane was getting lighter, but not airborne, when we crossed the big white runway numbers. We rattled into the gravel overrun, and with a couple of skips, the plane struggled to lift off. The gear came up as we cleared the fence at the base boundary by only a couple of feet, and the engines continued to scream until we had a safe airspeed. With flaps adjusted and throttles back a little, we were suddenly back to a routine flight.

Doug looked at Izer and said simply, "That's what overruns are for, right?" He leaned forward to adjust his seat, and I saw that his flight suit was soaked across his back. In fact, mine was too!

It would be another boring flight around the 200-mile long N/S imaginary racetrack 200 miles offshore. At 8,000 feet over San Francisco, we were startled when an overinflated Mickey Mouse balloon appeared out of nowhere and zipped over the right wing. Mickey's transparent cheeks were puffed up like he would explode in just a few more feet of altitude.

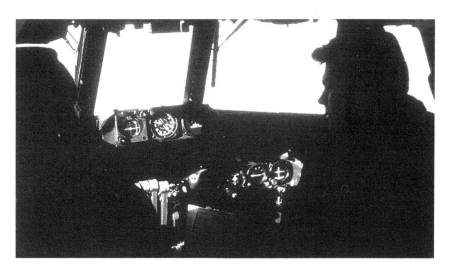

Pilot (L) and copilot peer out of the windscreen of an RC-121D
in 1959 during the International Geophysical Year (IGY).

As we crossed the Faralons, I unbuckled my jump seat to go back to my radar crew—who, by now, would be warming up their equipment.

As I shuffled behind the flight engineer (the cockpit of the C-121 is shoehorn tight), he touched my elbow and said, "Hey, Lieutenant, you're a geologist, aren't you?"

"Uh . . . yes," I answered, with considerable surprise.

"What do you make of these?" he asked as he passed me a small bottle of chicken bouillon cubes.

When I touched the bottle, I knew it was not bouillon cubes. The little jar weighed at least ten ounces—and was only half full. I looked curiously at the flight engineer. He nodded approvingly at me, so I unscrewed the cap and looked in. The stuff was about pea-gravel size and smaller and metallic yellow in color. I looked a little closer and asked him, "Are they?"

"They are!" He could hardly contain his grin.

"Hey, I have to go to work," I pleaded. "What are you doing in about two hours?"

"I'll come back to your place after we get on station—okay?"

"Okay, but don't forget. Promise?"

"It's a promise," he said.

As soon as we got on station, things got messy in a hurry. A westbound B-47 we were tracking flew directly above us at over 30,000 feet. The pilot called us on our frequency and chatted with us briefly. He was squawking a solid signal on his transponder, and we could see his position even in the middle of the sea clutter that jams the radar returns for a few miles around our location above the water. When he had cleared the forty-mile sea clutter, we could see his aircraft echo as well as the telltale identifier "squawk." As we plotted his course along our big operations map, we lost radio contact with Hamilton (our control center, just north of San Francisco). After spotty reporting for a while, we finally gave up trying to tell them he was still on course as he left our radar coverage. I slouched down into my console chair, noted the nearly blank operations map, and checked my watch. Then I began thinking about gold nuggets—big ones and lots of them!

After a quiet interlude, an airman watching the west edge of our coverage broke the silence to tell the board workers the position and direction of an eastbound target. Chavez calmly said, "He's not scheduled!"

Two sweeps of the antenna and Chavez called Hamilton to give them our "unknown" at KR PN, angels 24, heading 092 degrees.

"Say again, 6288." Hamilton's signal was buzzing with static, and we understood him only because we hear the phrase "say again" all the time, for a host of reasons.

We could give only two more positions to Hamilton before we lost the target (now a true "bogey") in our sea clutter.

I called on the intercom: "Pilot, this is Radar."

"Go ahead, Radar." It was Izer talking.

"We have an unknown passing directly above us, eastbound at about 24,000."

"We're between decks of clouds, we can't see anything," Izer reported.

More tries with the radios. More static. We could not even tell if Hamilton knew we were trying to call. We tried changing the volume, again, and all other tricks of the game, but nothing helped. The IGY had us beaten.

The airman watching the south area of our coverage then said, "We have a line of bright patches in the sea clutter heading off toward LA. Somebody's dropping chaff!"

"Good eyes, Larry," Chavez said. "Wake up, guys!"

A couple of the console operators leaned more directly over their tympani-sized scopes. Our "unknown" target was dropping strips of foil to confuse our radar eyes. In the sea clutter, we would never have spotted him if the chaff had not been dropped in clusters. "We've got another one heading for Seattle!" squeaked Randy, who had not said a word for over an hour, and his voice had trouble working clearly. He was covering the north sector.

Chavez and I were trying all the mikes and frequencies, trying to reach Hamilton. No success!

"Uh-oh! More to the east," I said, "heading right for Frisco."

The flight engineer with his bouillon bottle came to my console just then.

"We're having a bad time right now, so you and I will have to wait," I said, somewhat desperately.

As we spoke, Chavez left his mike and walked over to my console and pointed out another line of bright spots beginning to appear, heading for the general area of Portland.

"Lieutenant, we gotta do something!" Chavez said.

We had been taking turns with different mikes, trying to reach Hamilton. Now our plot board had four red tracks (unknowns) heading toward several million people, and we couldn't tell anyone! We were on the edge of panic! Our status board showed a westbound flight north of us, but closer to land and much higher than we were.

"Sarge, who is this guy?" I asked Chavez. I was pointing to our plot of the plane on the big board. Within a couple of seconds, Chavez told me it was TWA flight 81, heading for Hawaii at 28,000. "Let's call him," I said. "He's higher and a lot closer to Hamilton."

"Go ahead," Chavez said.

"TWA 81, this is Air Force 6288, over."

With a little delay, maybe to get off the intercom button and onto transmit mode, we heard: "Uh . . . Air Force 6288, this is TWA 81."

It was the monotone voice of an old veteran pilot—seldom any excitement.

"Uh Roger, 81, this is 6288. We have a bit of a problem. We have too much static down here to call Hamilton Field. We need to relay some information to them. Can you help us?"

"Uh Roger, 6288. What's the message?"

"Try this, 81." I gave him the frequency for Hamilton Control and said: "We have an unknown at RH PP heading 127 degrees at 480 knots."

The voice of the TWA 81 pilot suddenly became much more attentive. "Uh, say again, 6288?"

"We have an unknown at RH PP heading 127 degrees at 480 knots."

"Roger, 6288. Is that RH PP heading 127 degrees at 480 knots?"

"Affirmative, 81. See if you can send it."

Our flight engineer could see we had something serious going on, so he picked up Hartshorn's headset and settled into the console seat. The tube was on, so he tried to figure out what we were doing. A full minute passed, but it seemed like an hour. Chavez was standing by his console, his headset cord stretched to the limit, looking at me with an expression approaching terror. I tried to ignore the other dozen pairs of eyes watching me.

"Uh . . . 6288, this is TWA 81."

"Go ahead, 81."

"Hamilton reads us 5 by 5 and got a copy."

"Thanks, 81. There's more. We have an unknown at RP ZT heading 022 at 475 knots, over."

"We copy another unknown at RP ZT heading 022 at 475 knots."

"That's a Roger, 81, and another at RR ZS heading 008 at 475 knots, over."

"That's RR ZS heading 008 at 475 knots? Over."

"Roger, 81," I started.

Chavez cut in quickly, "And another at RR AS heading 084 at 485 knots." He had plotted the one I spotted heading east.

The TWA pilot confirmed our last position report and said, "Uh, 6288, stand by one."

After a good four minutes, we heard: "Air Force 6288, this is TWA 81, over."

"This is 6288," I replied anxiously.

"They have all four plots, can we help any more?"

"Affirmative, 81. We'll give a follow-up position in about ten minutes, okay?"

"That's a Roger, 6288."

The console operators all looked at me. This looked pretty serious, to say the least. What was going on? Did I know something they did not? This was no longer a routine flight.

"Pilot, this is Radar," I called.

"Go ahead, Radar."

"Have you been listening to us back here?"

"Uh . . . yeah."

"Doug, do you know anything about this that I don't?" I asked.

"Nope."

"These are good plots. Let's hope it is a practice penetration."

Doug told us that he and Izer had been trying to pick up some civilian band radio for a late newscast, but there was mostly static and no clues. None of the few pilots in range of our radios were saying anything unusual.

We made our next position reports to TWA 81, and they reported that Hamilton got them all, but it took several repeats to get the last one. Eighty-one could hear Hamilton, but Hamilton was losing 81.

A full hour passed before a C-130 outbound from Travis Air Force Base (San Francisco) came up on our status board. As soon as we got two sweeps on the radar to show him on his proper course, speed, and altitude, I called him.

"Air Force 4191, this is Air Force 6288, over."

"Go ahead, 6288, this is 4191."

"How's the weather at San Francisco?" I asked, trying to avoid any hint of our recent experience. "Our radios are pretty bad today."

"Well, Frisco is having a great sunset now. Maybe some fog moving in from Point Reyes, but it is pretty thin so far, over."

"Thanks, 4191. Have a good flight," I said.

Our entire crew gave a deep sigh, and a lot of tense shoulders eased back in their seats. I could see a dozen relaxed men.

Chavez and I agreed that our outbound B-47 was probably four B-47s with only one squawking on the transponder. They got out of range and came back over us without squawking and split over our sea clutter. If they had not dropped chaff, we might have missed them—especially the one headed for San Francisco. We hoped that Air Defense fighters had enough time to make intercepts on the four bogeys.

Chavez and I complimented the men on a great job. Doug left Izer on the controls and came back to talk to us about our very unusual mission. When he finished, he went back to the bunks for a nap.

The flight engineer, Master Sergeant Duncan, rattled his "bouillon" at me, and the two of us went to a bench in the rear—after heating up TV dinners out of the galley. Duncan was handsome, well-tanned, and muscular. He had a lot of dark hair sneaking up to the open neckline of his flight suit.

"Do you remember Sergeant Watts?" he started. "The one with the pipe that took my flight last Tuesday?"

"Yes, I met him," I said, "but we didn't talk much."

"We've got a real hot spot for gold," he said.

"Where? Tell me about it," I said.

"We use scuba gear and work in the plunge pool below a small waterfall," he said as he pulled a leather cord out of the zipper pocket over his right chest. The cord had a ten-power B&L hand lens looped through it as a loose necklace, typical of field gear for a geologist or biologist. He dumped the "bouillon" nuggets out on the coarse khaki canvas on the bench and handed me the lens.

I twisted to the side a little so that the light was right behind my ear, and I looked intensely at a couple of the bigger nuggets.

"How long did it take you to gather these?" I asked, turning over the one that looked like half of a cashew nut.

"Three days, once we found the right spot. Watts has almost this many too."

The nuggets were well rounded and highly polished, typical of gold that had travelled a good distance in a tumbling stream. The pounded, split cashew would be worth a good $20 in gold, maybe $50 as a showpiece. The little nuggets were battered. They get rather flattened in transit when they are smaller than these. Pebbles and cobbles pound the gold when the spring runoff stirs up the rocks on the bottom of a stream. The smaller stuff becomes flakes after a few miles of tumbling downstream in the mountains.

"Are there more of these?" I asked as I pointed to a couple of the larger ones.

"I think so," Duncan said. "Watts and I are going out again when I get home from this flight."

"Where is the place?" I asked innocently.

He gave me a suspicious look and said, "I won't tell you where it is, but it is less than three hours from my house."

He leaned closer to me so I could hear him better, above the noisy drone of four big engines on our Super Connie. "The plunge-pool is in smooth granite. The best chunks are coming out of cracks in the granite. We 'snipe' them out with coat-hanger wires. We're going to use wet suits this time so that we can stay down longer. The water is icy cold."

I handled all the nuggets in the chicken bouillon container. Well, to be honest, I *fondled* all the nuggets from the container. I must admit that I have a great fondness for natural gold. Correction: I have a great fondness for any kind of gold. I put the nuggets back in the bouillon bottle and told him, "Your chicken bouillon is now gold bullion!"

Duncan and I talked a little more about the nuggets and the scuba diving to recover them. I would be seriously interested in doing some of the same kind of work, but with a family and three kids and no experience with scuba gear and not knowing where they were getting the gold, the idea soon faded into the noisy drone of the airplane. Maybe, I mused, after I get the air force out of my life, I can get more aggressive with my gold dreams.

Returning to Sacramento after a long night and day patrolling the skies.
Below is San Francisco in the afternoon sun from about ten thousand feet.

Our next flight assignment was about four days later, and Master
Sergeant Duncan had been out again with Watts. They used wet suits this
time, and they recovered even more gold, although he didn't bring me any
samples to see. Then I got a temporary assignment to give some weather
briefings to other crews on the "early warning radar" flights in the Super
Connies, and I lost track of Duncan when he was moved to another crew.

About three weeks passed before I was briefing my old crew again
for a night take-off. Master Sergeant Duncan was there, and we had a
brief chance to talk. He was having a falling out with Watts, and they
hadn't made any more sorties together to the "gold waterfall." I think
they were starting to work alone because they were not on the same crew
and, therefore, not available on the same days to go sniping for gold.

My enlistment in the US Air Force was about to end, and they
moved me out of the flight crews because I would be discharged before I
became fully qualified as a pilot in the RC-121. It was a tough transition
program, and the plane has a lot of equipment to become proficient
with. I really enjoyed the flying and practice landings. We had several
military bases to practice on, and we had a special day in San Francisco
Bay where we practiced escaping from a C-121 that we could "ditch" in
the bay and get away in life rafts. We were very much aware of the fact

that "ditching" a C-121 carcass that was suspended on cables near the shore of San Francisco Bay was different from a panicked crew crashing in high seas on a stormy night two hundred miles out in the Pacific; but the training was very necessary for our confidence in the buoyancy of the airplane.

Anyway, in my last couple of weeks as a "lame duck" weather-briefing officer, our original crew had a party, and they invited me to join them. I was anxious to talk with flight engineer Duncan that had the chicken bullion. He wouldn't talk to me much, and I could tell it was a pretty emotional subject. But there was a lot of beer and plenty of loud talk and war stories about aborted missions and a few actual crashes that some of the crew had been close to or were actually on board. Finally, a little after midnight, when part of the crew had actually gone home, Duncan opened up with "The Rest of the Story."

It turns out that Master Sergeant Watts was a bit of a hot-tempered single man who had a lovely girlfriend. When the two would meet at Watts's house for a scuba trip, Duncan seemed to take extra notice of his girlfriend. The girl did not push him away either, but there was never any real reason for Watts to be concerned about Duncan. At least, he *claimed* there was nothing to their relationship. But there was a relationship with a crew member from a T-29 (a plane used to train navigators in the USAF). Some T-29s were based at Mather Field, also near Sacramento. Watts didn't trust Duncan, and he openly accused him of messing around with his girlfriend. There was some messing around, but it was with another guy from Mather. One day when they were sniping gold, there was a serious confrontation and Watts pushed Duncan, and he went sprawling into the river. Nobody is sure that Watts intended to push him into the river, but it could have been a very serious situation. Fortunately, Duncan was not seriously hurt, and he was a strong swimmer and got out safely. But the gold-sniping relationship was definitely over. Two days later, when Watts's crew was flying out over the Pacific, Duncan drove to a brass foundry near Stockton, California, and got about twenty pounds of brass welding scraps, mostly shiny little beads that had fallen on the floor of the shop. He drove to the golden waterfall and tossed all the brass drippings into the stream. Some he took above the waterfall and some he took quite a distance downstream, so that any gold would be hard to find among all the look-alike chunks of brass. The scuba mine abruptly ceased operation.

RAGS TO RICHES

In the spring of 1965, my graduate program at Washington State University had sunk to its lowest ebb. While checking the field samples for my thesis, I became painfully certain that I could not finish by June commencement. My assistantship would run out June 1, and my family of five would have no income. I still had more than half of the mountain of samples left to check under the binocular microscope before I could start writing the dissertation. I sat alone in a musty old lab. Much of the light in the room was from a tiny bulb focused on the sample under the microscope. Outside, it was raining under dismal skies. The basement of old Morrill Hall was downright depressing. Even the somber wet basalt blocks, used for outside window trim, added to my discouragement.

The author, when younger, sits among his hundreds
of rock samples collected on thesis work from a dozen
research sites in Colorado, Wyoming, and Utah.

I looked around at the battered cardboard boxes of field samples that I had collected nearly two years before. LAKETOWN CANYON, VERMILLION CREEK, and JONES HOLE sections were finished, but I still had eight others in addition to the 130 trays of WHITEROCKS RIVER samples laid out before me on the table. The pile of gaudy homemade sample bags mocked my mood of depression. My mind drifted back to the church painting project and how my wife, Sherry, had agreed to save a few dollars by sewing several thousand sample bags out of the extra paint rags. I could no longer hold back the tears. She had been so cheerful and encouraging for so long. She was the only one—including the geology faculty—that never doubted that I would get a PhD. Twelve years of school! "For better or worse," in her case, was becoming an awful lot of "worse."

I mopped up a few tears from the table and dried my eyes. I had to get after this section and finish the job for her sake if nothing else. With a deep sigh, I started: "Sample no. 1, Whitcrocks River Section, Utah." And with a little renewed vigor, I plowed back into the job of upgrading the scrawled notes from my field notebook. The descriptions passed up through the Cambrian-Mississippian unconformity into my familiar "Madison" limestone; and when I slid sample no. 17 under the scope, I was startled to see, gleaming under the light, a pea-sized cavity filled with brown sphalerite. I checked the field notebook and was relieved to see that I had noticed this occurrence of high-grade zinc sulfide. The description in the notebook brought back the memory of that morning in the Whiterocks River Canyon when I had considered the potential that the area had for an ore deposit. I was near the South Uinta Fault, which often contains some low-grade mineralization. Good sphalerite, however, was a real teaser. But for now, there was no time to waste daydreaming; so I recorded the occurrence of sphalerite and went on to the next sample.

The next day, after teaching a lab in the morning, I went back to the basement and plunged into the scope work again. By now, the samples were from the section near the contact with the Humbug Sandstone, and I was taking extra pains to catch any hint of an unconformity at the base of the sand. Sample no. 82 was next. As I slid the tray toward the scope, I could see it was coarse-grained, crumbly sandstone of some sort. It was sand all right, but composed of angular grains of clear calcite and some scattered quartz. It also had many tiny flecks of what looked for all the world like gold! Could it be gold? There was so much of it that my pulse rate immediately surged, and the thoughts of the sphalerite mineralization on the South Uinta Fault returned. Had I found a fossil-placer concentration of gold on an unconformity from a nearby lode? Ancient movement and mineralization on the South Uinta Fault! What an incredible find! With a steel probe, I scraped a fleck loose and mashed it under the point. Yes, *very* soft and malleable. The color and luster were perfect. It had to be gold. And *lots of it*! If I could find fifteen flecks or so out of this little walnut-sized sample, a ton of this stuff would hold a fortune. Still, I couldn't believe it. I dug out two more flakes to test in a cylinder of the heavy liquid bromoform. Never had I seen grains sink so fast. They didn't just settle in the heavy liquid; they plummeted! I knew I had gold. I tried a blowpipe to test the melting point. It was perfect. Gold—it was GOLD!

Carefully I hid the sample boxes and notebooks so that no one could link the gold with the Whiterocks River section. It would be easy for someone to find my thesis proposal to learn where my samples were collected, but that information would not be very helpful to someone if they did not know which one of my dozen sites contained the gold.

When I had the room "safe," I called in a fellow grad student from New York, Joe Ruzicka. He sensed my excitement and eagerly peered through the microscope. After mashing a little grain with the steel probe, he asked where the sample came from. I told him it was one of my thesis samples, but I did not tell him which area was the source. I assured him it was not a prank. I confided that I had tested the melting point with a blowpipe and the density with bromoform. I was convinced it was gold.

Joe was convinced too. Excitedly, he dug $10 out of his billfold and slapped it on the table. "This is all I've got on me—but I can get more," he said. "Count me in! I'll help in any way you need."

I told him to relax, and if I needed help, I would include him.

Next, I shared the sample with Dave McIntyre, who was the mineralogy lab teacher. He was a little sharper on minerals than the rest of us. His first concern was whether the gold was *on* the sample or *inside* the sample. He finally concluded that a fleck or two were definitely under those transparent crystals.

Then Dr. Mills, the geology chairman, came in; but by this point, the sample was nearly destroyed. With his experience in gold mines in Canada, he quickly concurred that it was *gold*.

Now, I faced a problem. Could I sit on the knowledge that there was an unclaimed gold deposit on the Whiterocks River long enough to get a PhD, or should I go immediately to the field and start on the deposit and hope that the geology department would accept some more delays in my graduate program? I checked some maps of Utah and found that the deposit was on open US Forest Service land. It was close to an Indian reservation but still safely in legal "prospecting country." I did not dare wait. Already, a dozen good geologists had seen my gold. It wouldn't take much of a sleuth to get my thesis proposal and figure out where I had been working. I made the decision to call my dad and arrange to meet him in the field, and we would stake the claims immediately. It would be an exciting project for the two of us to work together. If this put my PhD in jeopardy, I would have to risk it. This was the break of a lifetime, and if it was one-tenth as good as it looked, I certainly would never need a PhD!

While my mind began organizing the trip back to the outcrop (and spending a few million dollars), I went back to the basement of old Morrill Hall. I looked one more time at the crumbled sample. I poked around in the debris, looking for one more speck of gold. Finding none, I rummaged around for the empty sample bag, hoping some gold had been trapped in the cloth as in the "Golden Fleece" of ancient times. When I finally found sack no. 82, my gold mine suddenly caved in— crushing me and my dreams.

The sack for sample no. 82 was sewn from a strip of turquoise-colored silk that had once been a beautiful ceremonial sari worn by a foreign student from India. Its beautiful flowered pattern was printed with very fine, but very genuine, gold powder.

Fabric from a ceremonial "sari" from India is decorated with real gold dust.

Another dozen bags were made from that same printed cloth, but for some devilish coincidence, the first one to be seen with a microscope was the basal sand on the unconformity near the South Uinta Fault where the speck of high-grade zinc mineral was found. The gold dust would be brushed off easily from almost every other sample. But sample no. 82 was a porous, granular calcite grit—possibly the only sample of my entire thesis that could have fooled me. And it sure did!

HURRICANES AND CLAMS

During my seven years with Exxon in Texas, I ran into a couple more treasures. While stationed in Corpus Christi with Humble Oil's South Texas Division, I spent many days at Padre Island National Seashore. I also hunted ducks on the west shore of Laguna Madre. Padre Island is actually a barrier island with a lagoon over a hundred miles long between the island and the mainland of South Texas. In the fall, ducks migrate constantly along the lagoon, especially along the west shore. I found that I could crouch down in a few weeds and grass and get some pretty good shooting there, even without any decoys. Blustery, wet days were best. On several occasions, after daylight savings ended, I could drive to the site and get about half an hour of hunting and still get to work on time. Of course, on Saturday I could stay longer if the birds were flying.

My family enjoyed going over the causeway and entering Padre Island National Seashore where we could play in the surf in the open Gulf of Mexico. The shoreline there is beautiful and goes the whole length of the island—one hundred miles of uninterrupted beach. The beach is gentle enough that one can wade out perhaps a hundred feet, and often there was a shallow bar out that far, and one could stand up and even fish the slightly deeper water outside the bar. We spent much time there, and I swam many hours outside that bar. However, I stopped swimming out in the open ocean after I saw the movie *Jaws*.

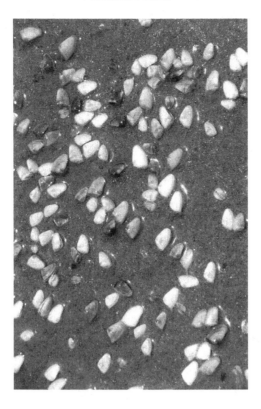

Mostly live *Donax* clams on Padre Island, Texas. They are a little over half an inch in size (15 mm). Image courtesy of the staff at Padre Island National Seashore (2013).

On one family outing, there had been some storms out in the Gulf of Mexico, and the heavy surf had uncovered a tremendous mass of a small colorful clam called *Donax*. The shells are less than an inch long, and hardly worth the bother to try to harvest them. However, they were clams, and they were very abundant. Using a screen to remove the sand, I collected several gallons of the clams and took them home. I rinsed them repeatedly in cold water to get most of the sand out, and then I boiled about a pint of the shells to see what would happen. In the hot water, the shells all popped open, and by swirling the clams around in a strainer I was able to separate most of the meat from the shells. They tasted about the same as clam strips you might get at a restaurant. When I finished with my bucket of clams, I had about two quarts of very tasty clams. My processing was not perfect because there were a few stray grains of sand in the finished product.

In September of 1967, Hurricane Beulah came ashore between Brownsville and Corpus Christi. The fury on Padre Island was violent enough to breach Padre Island in several places and flood seawater into the hypersaline Laguna Madre. When big storms flood into Laguna Madre, fish and other creatures that live in the open sea can survive in Laguna Madre for months and even years until the channel is blocked again and the excess evaporation and limited inflow allow the lagoon to become too salty for most of the organisms to survive. Many less sensitive critters survive and even thrive in the extra salty water.

When Beulah smashed ashore, my neighborhood in Corpus Christi received minor damage, and I went out a few days later to see what had happened to Padre Island. There was a lot of seaweed in many areas, and I saw numerous white jellyfish "bladders." I am not sure what part of the jellyfish they were, but when the jellyfish is washed ashore, the white bags would puff up about the size of a softball. And when I drove along the beach, I could not avoid all of them; and when I ran over one, it made a loud pop. It was a novelty, and I entertained my kids a little by popping the bags as I drove down the beach. My only worry was that I might get careless and get stuck in the sand. The area we were driving in was almost devoid of other cars. We were hoping to find another bunch of *Donax* clams.

I drove south several miles and was about to run out of daylight when I saw a chunk of badly weathered wood sticking out of the sand. I stopped to kick it and see if it was small enough to pick up. It was solid and did not budge. Briefly I wondered about the old timber, trying to guess what it might have been. I climbed back in the car, and as the kids were getting restless, I knew I needed to head back to our home in Corpus Christi. I turned the car around, and as I studied the sand to make sure I was moving into packed sand where I would not get stuck, I caught a glimpse of something rather odd and stopped the car to look down at the object. It was two shiny little discs that were touching each other. My first thought was a buckle or maybe buttons. I opened the door and reached down to pick them up. They were heavy and metallic, looking somewhat like pewter. The light was getting dim, but I could see a cross pattern on one of them; and it was quite distinct. I rubbed the better one on the seat cover, and it became brighter, and I guessed it might be silver. As a geologist, I always have a hand lens with me, and I got one out of the glove box and looked. The print was bold and Spanish. *Peru* and *1541* were distinct, along with a few words I didn't recognize. I stuffed them in my pocket and drove on home, not knowing what I had found. I noted the mileage from my discovery to the pavement near the causeway was 26.4 miles.

When I got home, I called my librarian friend who knew a lot about the history of the Karankawa Indians that had lived on parts of Padre Island in the recent past. He said the Indians were smart enough to dig water wells on Padre Island because often there is a lens of freshwater under the island that results from rainfall. The entire island is loose sand, and the groundwater near the beaches is salty; but if the island has enough relief and is wide enough, freshwater is possible in many areas. Then my librarian friend mentioned some shipwrecked sailors that perished from thirst because there was no freshwater to be found on the surface of the island. I dug my two discs out of my pocket and described the one with *Peru* and *1541* on it. He asked what color it was, and I told him it was probably silver.

"That's a Spanish real!" he said. "Much of the Spanish coinage of the old colonial days was gold and sometimes silver reals. There were many varieties, but they all had the same value. In the old sailing days, English dollars were supposed to be exchangeable with the real pieces of eight and the Spanish doubloons."

"Where did you get it? he said.

"I think we need to talk," I said. "Can I come over?"

As I drove up to his house, Pat Murphy came out of the side door of his big garage. The inside of the garage had excellent lighting with a large desk on the back end, and the walls were lined all the way to the ceiling with books. He was a very experienced book collector, and on more than one fishing trip with him, we had stopped at a garage sale and picked up a couple of old books. He would pay 25 cents or maybe a dollar or two for some nondescript book—and when he was back with me, he would tell me that one was a first printing of a now-famous writer, or possibly a research paper about some little-known South Texas history. I remembered the day he got the little paperback about Karankawa Indians. He had hundreds of *National Geographic* magazines all neatly arranged on one wall of the garage. He said, "Any *National Geographic* would be worth at least a quarter to somebody, sometime. A few good issues were worth many dollars."

I tested him once by asking if he had a copy of the August 1958 issue. He quickly located the correct shelf and pulled down a copy. The magazine looked as good as new.

"What is so special about this issue?" he asked.

I took the magazine and flipped to an article entitled "The Case of the Bogus Coffin" and showed it to him.

This was a story of a coffin that was shipped from Egypt back in the 1930s. Some scoffers of the procedure of radiometric dating had asked some Ivy League geophysicists how old the wood was from the coffin. They did not tell the scientists where the wood came from. The age of a splinter from the lid was determined to be only thirty years or so. When the scientists were told that they were way wrong, they tried a second sample from the lid, which was also the approximate same age—quite recent. The scoffers told them that the age of the samples was very wrong and that the geophysicists didn't know what they were doing. The scientists told them that the samples they just tested were only a few years old, and they needed to get a better sample if the tests seemed to be wrong. A third sample—this time from the bottom of the coffin—was tested, and the age came up over two thousand years old.

It seems the coffin was sent on a ship that encountered a storm, and the lid was damaged during the voyage to America. The people selling the coffin had hired some wood specialists to fabricate a new lid to look like the damaged one. The coffin was very old, but the lid was modern wood. Radiometric dating works!

Now back to the Spanish reals. We walked back to the desk, and he pulled up a folding chair for me to sit by him at the desk. I placed the two coins on the desk. He looked at them with delight and took a large reading glass from a drawer in the desk.

"Aaaahh, YES!" he exclaimed, "these are great specimens. Now, where did you get them?"

I told him the story of my trip down Padre Island to check if any breaches crossed the island to open a channel to Laguna Madre. I told him that I popped a number of jellyfish bladders while driving along and found an old timber poking out of the sand. When I told him that I spotted the coins when I turned around to come home because it was getting late, he asked me if anyone else was down there.

"No, I don't think so. There were a lot of people up near the causeway, but I don't remember anybody down there the last couple of miles."

"We have a problem because you cannot collect anything important in a National Seashore. Everything on the island belongs to the government. I would suggest that you not go back down there."

I drove home, planning to "not go back down there"—but my mind began to conjure up scenes of broken chests full of Spanish coins and jewelry littering the beach about 26.4 miles from the pavement at the end of the causeway at Padre Island National Seashore. I could not sleep. About six a.m., I quietly left the house and drove across the causeway and headed south to my treasure at 26.4 miles south of the pavement. It was a bright, sunny day, and I wished that I had left the house at three a.m. instead of six.

When the odometer indicated I was at 24.9 miles, I could see some activity ahead. There were a couple of green Park Service cars and some black four-door sedans. I slowed a bit, and as I got closer, I saw some men stringing up a bunch of orange crime-scene tape from the area where I had seen the weathered timber all the way down to the waterline. Two men in swimsuits were driving some rebar rods in the shallow water. A couple of black timbers poked out of the water near the men. I had not seen the timbers in the water the night before, but I had been looking for jellyfish and *Donax* clams on the sandy beach.

"Whoa," I told myself. "I still have those two coins in my pocket. If some bright federal officer saw my tracks where I picked up those coins, he will be able to identify my tire marks. Maybe even the marks of the coins in the sand."

I stopped the car and slowly headed back up the beach to the north. I unbuckled my seat belt and fumbled around in my pocket until I found the coins and stuffed them under the passenger seat of the car. I drove slowly, but broke out in a cold sweat. I met two more Park Service cars headed south. It was going to be a busy day back at the shipwreck. I got home before nine a.m. and have kept my two reals out of sight since then. So much for broken chests of coins and jewels.

TREASURE NUMBER 8

MICROPALEONTOLOGY

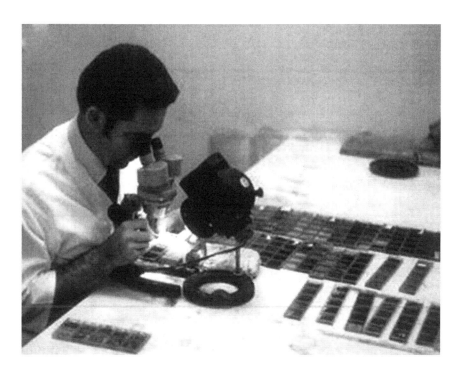

"Running samples" from a well in Texas. The drill bit grinds up the
rock, and the "cuttings" are flushed to the surface in the drilling
mud. The geologist can recognize the formations and checks
for fossils and traces of hydrocarbons among the cuttings.

The author trying to correlate electric well logs from an area in Texas.

The author implies that discovering a gas well in Texas is a "cinch."

Another path in my lifelong quest for treasure and fortune drifted into paleontology. Humble Oil and Refining Company (an early part of Exxon) hired me as an exploration geologist in Texas in the 1960s. Some of my training and work involved "picking bugs," or gathering microfossils out of the drill cuttings and mud that come up through the drill pipe as an oil well is drilled. A good paleontologist usually can tell what formation the drill is cutting by the small chunks of rock and tiny fossils they may contain. To "run the cuttings" on a well, a geologist may check the samples every five or ten feet—or, in critical areas, every foot—in order to determine how far the drill bit has penetrated into the rock formations. On a deep well (say 20,000 feet), there may be several hundred little trays of washed cuttings, and the geologist—or a more specialized micropaleontologist—might look at the cuttings under a microscope for days and even weeks depending on what sort of problem is being solved.

This is *Textularia* as illustrated in a report from the 1890s. Remember, he is only as big as a grain of sand. There are many species of *Textularia,* and they have been around millions of years.

When I was with Exxon in the Corpus Christi, Texas, office, a friend of mine named Kennard Harper was the company's expert on *Textularia warreni* variety 18. At the time, I could recognize *Textularia* (which is about the size of a grain of sand)—but to pick a *Tex. warreni* was beyond my ability, let alone *Tex. warreni* 18. Variety 18 probably had a little whumpus on its glooper instead of the normal rodelei. I couldn't even identify the rodelei, let alone the glooper or whumpus. (Of course, these terms substitute for company classified information because this stuff was pretty valuable along the Gulf Coast in the 1960s.

I have substituted phony words.) Harper was good enough that when he was sitting down with us for the birthday dinner for his twin girls, the phone rang and he picked it up.

"This is Harper," he said, then "Yes . . . yes . . . ah, yes . . . Okay."

He hung up the phone, walked over and kissed his wife, and picked up a small briefcase and a microscope case on the way to the door and was gone. Happy birthday, kids! An offshore Exxon oil rig was about to reach a section of potential reservoir rock with high-pressure gas and/or oil. If they drilled into it too fast, the gas may push the mud column out of the well, and there was a high probability of a disastrous blowout. They wanted to drill as close and fast as possible with low-weight mud and then set steel casing before drilling ahead into the danger zone.

In those days, the cost of the rig alone was over $35,000 per day plus all the crew, etc. Ken's job was to drive to the airport and meet a helicopter that would get him to the offshore rig, and he would immediately check the latest sample to come up the drill pipe. He would carefully look at any *Textularias* in the cuttings, often turning them over or propping them up to check the aperture or maybe the initial whorl. All this on a fossil critter the size of a sand grain mixed with, or imbedded in, one of the little rock chips. When *Tex. warreni* appeared, he would tell the driller to drill ahead slowly, and he would monitor the cuttings every few minutes. Eventually, near the base of the safe formations (and that may take a few minutes or even days), the correct bugs would start to appear.

Ken would then stop the drilling, and the rig crew would spend a day or so pulling five miles of pipe out of the hole and set a thick cement plug in the hole. Then they would fill the hole with mud that would be heavy enough to prevent any high-pressure gas from blowing the mud column out of the hole. Next, a smaller bit would be lowered to the bottom of the hole, and it would drill through the plug and soon enter the gas/oil zone. If Ken was right, it wouldn't take long to get to the pay zone. If the exploration geologists and geophysicists had picked a good site to drill, they might complete an incredibly valuable well. If Ken was wrong, they may take way too much time to get there—or if he had not stopped them in time, they could have a blowout that might catch fire and cook a dozen men or so and destroy millions of dollars of equipment. We might have punched a hole into billions of dollars' worth of valuable hydrocarbons that would all be lost if the company could not put out the blowout.

These are some of the hazards of searching for treasure. For some reason, I think Ken's salary was more than mine; but I never asked. My fortune would not be in micropaleontology.

OTHER FOSSILS

A few marine fossils from the Honaker Shale of Paleozoic Age near Moab, Utah. They are characteristic of a shallow ocean environment.

Not all paleontology is so dramatic. One of our Exxon "bug pickers" heard of some larger fossils on a ranch by El Indio, Texas. I made some inquiries, and we got permission to go to the place and collect a fossil named *Sphenodiscus*. This critter was a disc-shaped cephalopod (like the pearly *Nautilus* but much thinner), about 90 million years old. The plan was to go out there early in order to collect in the morning to avoid the oppressive afternoon heat, which prevails along the Rio Grande in summer.

I picked up three fellow geologists in my old '62 Falcon four-door. We drove out in darkness and reached the ranch right after daylight.

A few miles later, we arrived at the desired location, just across the river from Mexico. Donning our backpacks for the expected treasure, some lunch and an ample supply of water, we headed out in the endless semiarid desert of cactus, mesquite, snakes, cactus, bugs, sparse grass, cactus, quail, and an occasional fossil cephalopod. Did I mention cactus? There were many kinds, and they all had stickers—some small and fuzzy, and others with long scary needles.

This is a composite print of the Cretaceous cephalopod
Sphenodiscus. The small image has a pen for scale. The larger
image shows more detail of the wiggly "suture lines." The suture
lines help to identify the genus and species of cephalopods.

In a few hours, we had our packs full. Everything from perfect discs the size of one's hand to pieces with excellent suture patterns preserved. There were several species too. In the back of my mind, I harbored the idea of someday teaching geology, as I was the only one on this venture with a doctorate degree in geology. I was thinking "lab specimens for paleontology." These were great examples, and I envisioned using some for trading for equally good specimens of other fossils. Satisfied with our haul, we ate lunch and lugged our booty back to the car.

This had been the perfect trip. The heat was only just now climbing into the hot range, and the car had a good A/C. No problems and superb specimens. We were delighted as we piled into the car. I hit the starter and heard *click*. The world got very quiet. When we arrived in the early morning, I had accidently left the lights on, and the battery was quite dead. Our happy mood went to total grim. We were many miles from the ranch house, even more miles from the tiny town of El Indio, and the Rio Grande blocked any venture into Mexico. We were getting low on water and out of food. The river was wet to be sure, although the water looked more like chocolate milk. The temperature was approaching 100 degrees, and it would get higher for the next few hours. Cell phones did not exist. I sensed that my pals were thinking: "What good is his fancy PhD if he is so stupid that he left the lights on?"

The little Falcon was pointed slightly downhill, and there was a big mound of dirt at the end of our little two-track road. The mound of dirt was only about a hundred feet away. A Falcon is a lightweight car, but it would be hard to push it uphill backward for a longer run.

"It might start if you can give me a good push," I said.

There were three skeptical looks. Somebody said, "What other choice is there?"

Somebody else said, "Not one that is any good."

I was glad that I had bought a cheap car instead of one with an automatic transmission. This old $600 used Falcon was about to be tested.

We reviewed the plan. Make sure the key is on. Make sure it is in neutral to start, and wait for the very last second to jam it into second gear (not first or third) and pop the clutch.

"Okay . . . Now, let's go!"

There were strained grunts from the right side, at the open back window, and from behind as the little car started forward. Some pebbles on the tracks seemed more like bricks, and the car was hopelessly slow at starting to move. Wait a little more . . . wait—and then I popped the clutch just before hitting the mound of dirt.

Varoooommm! The little Falcon leaped into action as if it would try to climb the mound of dirt. The gang quickly piled in, and we soberly contemplated what might have been. We had escaped another hazard of seeking treasure.

Collecting fossils can lead to other hazards. After moving to Colorado to teach in a small college in Grand Junction, I was picked to teach beginning paleontology. Alternate years I would take my paleo class on a field trip to the classic trilobite-collecting locality near Antelope Springs, which is partway into the House Range west of Delta, Utah. Trilobites are marine arthropods that had hard "shells" of chitin. They are distant relatives of crabs and came on the scene over 400 million years ago. Most critters did not have a hard shell much before that, and frankly, trilobites are rather handsome fossils. Paleontologists and amateur rock hounds love them. In the House Range, anyone can find trilobites, and the favorite is *Elrathia kingi*. In Wheeler Basin, there is a site where the Wheeler Shale, of middle Cambrian age, is loaded with good specimens. Access to the site often is restricted by the owner. I would get permission from him, and sometimes he would obligingly rip up a nice section for us to pick through the fresh stuff. It is very exciting to whack a slab of rock with a rock pick and have a perfect specimen pop out. Sometimes the fossil would come out, and other times, it would stick on one side of the slab and its cast would be on the "lid" side. I have been there often and have collected dozens.

A fine specimen of a trilobite collected from
the Wheeler Shale in western Utah.

Of course, this old prof has to check around the area for other genera in other layers. One rather windy day, I stopped in some lower formations, which were a little older than the Wheeler Shale. One trick is to turn over likely loose slabs of rock because there is as much chance for a good specimen to be on the bottom surface as there is on the exposed topside. The wind was causing a little trouble as I poked along the ledge, and I was not paying much attention to anything but keeping most of the dust out of my eyes. One nice slab I raised up to my knee in a half-crouch and flipped it over to find a perfect specimen about three inches long of the most beautiful, angry scorpion. Chalk up another hazard for hunting treasures.

GEM MINERALS

These golden topaz crystals were freshly removed from igneous rock at Topaz Mountain. The scale is about 80 percent of actual size. Sunlight will bleach the color out of the crystals in a few hundred years.

Topaz crystals from the slopes of Topaz Mountain, Utah. These
crystals may have been golden brown before sunlight bleached
them through thousands of years of exposure. They are near
actual size and show very little abrasion because they are harder
than quartz or most other grains common in sand.

Not far north of the House Range is Topaz Mountain, and my
trilobite trips always went there too. The molten rock that crystallized
there was just the right chemical composition to produce abundant
topaz crystals. An observant geologist will know when he is close to the
place if the sun is out, and he can see an excessive amount of sparkles
from the soil. Even at 50 mph, one can see sunlight glinting off the
crystal faces of *euhedral* topaz.

"Euhedral" means that the undamaged crystals have clean, angular
facets which make a unique crystal form. Most people are familiar with
euhedral quartz crystals with their six-sided prisms and pointed caps
on the end. Topaz crystals are similar; but to a mineralogist, they are
quite different.

At Topaz Mountain, some crystals may reach two inches in length,
but most are less than an inch. Crystals broken out of fresh rock samples
can be smoky or yellowish brown, but long exposure to sunlight bleaches
the color, and the crystals in the soil become perfectly clear. Topaz is

harder than quartz and only slightly softer than sapphire. The matrix rock weathers more easily than the topaz; so the hard, brilliant crystals are washed away from the crumbling rock and spread for thousands of years around the mountain by heavy spring runoff and occasional summer thunderstorms. The crystals are hard enough to keep their sharp angles and smooth facets undamaged even several miles from their origin. To collect the crystals, I would walk slowly while facing toward the sun and look for the glint of sunlight off the flat surfaces. They show up almost as bright as pieces of a broken mirror. I have found them at night with a near full moon using the same technique. My half-pound "treasure" of topaz crystals has very little value, but my experience with this lesser gemstone gets me into a problem in a later episode.

TREASURE NUMBER 9

THE GRAND CANYON

Descending the Bright Angel Trail seemed almost routine now after taking a dozen college classes to the bottom of the Grand Canyon. In spite of the trouble getting camping permits for fifteen students for every spring break, it really was a nice change of pace from the grind of daily classes. Besides, it's the best excuse I can think of to stay in shape. If I ever get too soft, I know that this canyon can kill me.

Bright Angel Trail gets muddy in the transition from deep snow at the top to hot desert at the bottom during spring break in March.

A pack train has just passed a group of hikers climbing out of the Grand
Canyon. They are in the Redwall Limestone, where the trail has been
blasted out of vertical cliffs. Hikers must stay on the outside of the trail as
the train passes so that the pack animals are not spooked over the edge.

A pack train was approaching me, and I stepped across a particularly
muddy part of the trail to find a stable perch on the outside of the trail.
That was the rule here: backpackers wait quietly on the outside of the
trail so that the mules won't get spooked over the side.

I waved at the old codger leading five mules loaded with duffle from
Phantom Ranch. He sure looked the part of a mule skinner. The guys
that get that job must have to pass an "authenticity test" to make sure
that they look like an old sourdough prospector or a cowpoke from a
nineteenth-century cattle drive. They add a lot of color for the dudes
that ride these trails in a saddle.

When the mules had passed, I noticed that the cloud level was
beginning to lift above the red Supai beds. Patches of sunlight appeared

off and on to the northwest. My promise of sunburn in the bottom of the canyon looked pretty certain now. As I admired the incredible view of the Redwall cliffs and the Tonto Bench spread before me, Les Stone and Hank Novak came around the corner and paused for a moment to talk with me.

"Which canyon is the campground in?" asked Les.

I pointed down to a notch on the far side of the gorge and said, "That's Bright Angel Canyon there—and it goes up behind all that Redwall there in the sun spot. It's only about five more miles."

"Do you still think the sun will shine on the bottom?" asked Hank, with a disbelieving look and a condemning voice.

"Didn't I promise sunburn?" I said with an obnoxious air of confidence. "The only reason we got four inches of snow on the rim is because I said it might happen."

"Yes, but you also said this hike would be fun, and my toes already hurt from being jammed into the front of my shoes all the way down."

"Aw, cheer up, Hank," I said. "Remember you get to hurt in all different places going out."

Ten miles of backpacking on a steep trail to the bottom of the Grand Canyon can be rough on shoes.

"Great, I can hardly wait." Hank turned and led Les on down the trail. He was limping noticeably on the left foot, but still moving rather fast. Les walked with a full spring in his step, and it made that silly twelve-inch gold pan swing from side to side as it dangled from his bulky pack. On some of the swings, the pan hit the pack frame, making an occasional noisy clank as Les went out of sight behind some boulders.

Les was the first of my students to bring a gold pan down here. I panned several spots on the Colorado River a couple of years back, but I didn't find enough "colors" to ever lug a gold pan down here again. I had told Les that there was very little gold in the river, but Les had the fever. I taught him to pan last summer, and now he took his gold pan almost every place he went.

Hikers emerge from the inner gorge of the Grand Canyon.
They have reached the sedimentary rocks of the Tapeats
Sandstone, much less than halfway to the top.

The day continued to brighten, and by the time I hit the switchbacks in the steep inner gorge, the sky was mostly clear and the trail was getting dusty. Two or three days of heavy storms are quickly forgotten when the sun starts to bake the bottom of the Grand Canyon.

A pack train is crossing the mule bridge at the bottom of
the Grand Canyon. The photo was taken from a switchback
on the trail in the inner gorge of the canyon.

As I crossed the mule bridge over the river, I noticed the time on my watch. I had been on the trail three hours and forty minutes. "About normal for me," I thought. If I skipped the scenery and photo stops, I could still make this trail in three hours with a pack on my back. "Maybe fifty years old is not so bad after all," I thought.

The campground near Phantom Ranch on Bright Angel Creek. Sixteen campers are crowded into the reserved site for our Mesa State College class here to study "The Geology of the Grand Canyon." A test will be given when they get back on top.

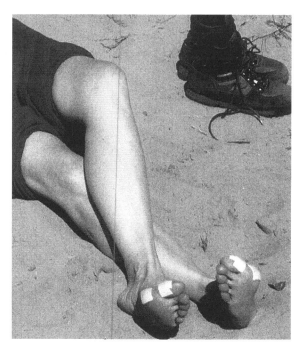

After a little first-aid, one weary hiker rests on the sandy beach near the camp on Bright Angel Creek.

By the time I reached the campground, my left ankle was really starting to ache, and I could feel a blister on the right big toe; but I walked into camp as sprightly as possible, hiding most of the limp and winces. Most of the students had already set up their tents and were in various stages of establishing a two-night camp. A couple of the girls had some nasty blisters—especially Mary, who was wearing a new pair of shoes. Four students were still missing, but at least two of them had stayed on top long enough to order breakfast at El Tovar Lodge. They had spent a cold night in the snow and were taking advantage of El Tovar's heating system.

At four forty, the last couple reached camp. Winston was recovering from a splitting headache, and his girlfriend had stayed back to give encouragement. The temperature was in the sixties, and the note at the ranger's signboard forecast scattered showers tomorrow and slightly cooler temperatures. "Well," I mused. "Not much sunburn for tomorrow, but the storm front must have passed through."

Macaroni and cheese was my supper menu, plus a box of chocolate pudding. But I grunted when I read the instructions on the box. "Add milk" it says. But I don't have milk! Rats!

Our college group was in good spirits with a minimum of real physical problems. Winston's headache faded as soon as he began nibbling at supper. Most of them had too much food, as usual. I keep telling myself to take no food to the bottom and eat the extras from the students. But if I ever did that, that would be the one year that the students would pack too lightly.

The macaroni and cheese was more than I needed, so I skipped the pudding and ate tomorrow's candy bar instead. I figured that I had earned it. While I was cleaning the macaroni mess out of my small aluminum pot, I made a mental note that macaroni and cheese was too messy for backpack cooking. Just then, Les Stone came down the trail. He was carrying something in his gold pan.

"I thought you said there was no gold in Bright Angel Creek," he started excitedly.

"Well," I countered, "I believe I said I didn't *think* there was any. I don't know of any gold mines on this drainage." (We geologists always try to have a way out if we make a mistake.)

He showed me the pan. There were two small flecks of gold all right, but they were very small.

"How close to the Colorado did you get it?" I asked.

"Above Phantom Ranch," Les said as he gestured toward the ranch.

"Well," I mused, "that's probably too far to have come from floods in the Colorado. Looks like you have proved that there is a source of gold in the Bright Angel drainage—whatever that is worth. Remember, it might be reworked from placer gold in the Tapeats Sandstone."

Les was not discouraged. He had found a trace of gold on a stream I didn't know about. It was an important coup for Les.

"Now, Les," I kidded, "go find some on a stream where you could legally file a claim."

Les took his pan back up the trail to pan some more. I watched him go, thinking how fun it would be to search for a deposit in one of the canyons near my home in Colorado. That's how it is done. Find a little gold on a creek that has no known deposit and search it out (if it has not been eroded away).

Both bridges are shown in this view looking
upstream in the inner gorge of the canyon.

This welcome sandy beach beneath the mule bridge at the bottom
of the Grand Canyon sometimes is missing when the carefully
controlled flow of the river washes away some of the sediment.

Three of us reserved a steak dinner for tomorrow night at Phantom
Ranch. A few drank some beer at the little canteen, but most of the
group was content to dangle their feet in the Colorado River at the big
sandbar below the ancient Anasazi pit houses. Our gang was all quiet
by 10:30 p.m. in our crowded group campsite.

The sky was blue when I looked out at 6:00 a.m. Sunburn City! Of
course, the canyon was magnificent. Soon, the early sunlight brought
the canyon up to its full splendor. Our group was up early with high
spirits; however, they all walked with various degrees of the "Bright
Angel Shuffle." Bruised or blistered feet plus traumatized calf muscles
(from putting on the brakes descending eight miles of steep trail) give
a peculiar gait to all but the expert hikers. Breakfast was over by eight
thirty, and the students were figuring out what to do for the full day
on the bottom.

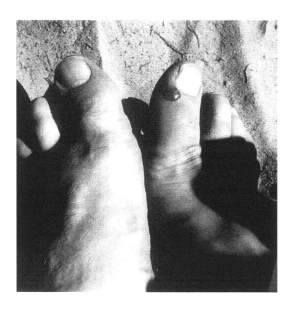

With two pairs of socks, the author usually avoided damage
to his feet. One sock must have developed a lump during
a steep ten-mile trail down to Phantom Ranch.

The Grand Canyon has plenty of ideal surgical tools for annoying blisters.

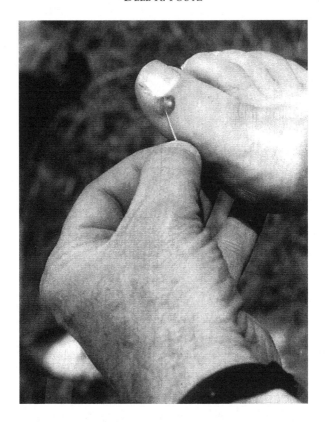

A blister is painlessly lanced with a cactus needle.

My ankle was good. I walked a few yards at a brisk pace, and my feet were okay. I had drained the small blister on my toe and changed to a pair of socks that did not crumple up under the toes. Nothing hurt, so I decided to hike up Bright Angel Creek to Cottonwood Campground. The round-trip would be about twelve miles, but with no backpack, I figured I could handle it. I asked around, but none of the students wanted to come along. That's okay. I usually waste too much time with rocks and photos for most students anyway.

I left camp about nine fifteen. My day "pack" was a bag of cookies, an orange, some granola bars, and a couple of carrots—all stuffed into an old plastic bread wrapper, which I tied to my belt. I carried a half-gallon water jug in one hand and my camera over the shoulder. I walked fast because I had already paid $16.50 for that steak I was going to eat at 5:00 p.m.

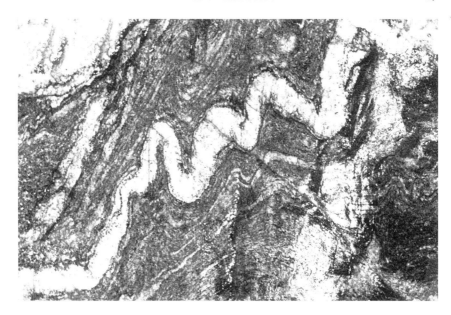

Ancient sedimentary rock layers have been heated and distorted at great depth and high pressures. This image from the Vishnu Schist at the bottom of the Grand Canyon reveals part of the story.

An hour into the trail, I noticed a lot of clouds, but they only added color to a beautiful scene. Bright Angel Canyon is very narrow and steep at the lower end. Magnificent dikes of pink granite cut at strange angles through vertical cliffs of dark metamorphic rocks. Huge feldspar crystals winked at me as they caught the scattered patches of sunlight. Boy, if there was a geologist's heaven on earth, this would be it. It really is the "Grand Canyon."

My hiking was brisk and a bit euphoric. I scarcely noticed a darkening overcast, but by about 11:00 a.m., I was in for a quick shower. "Scattered showers" the note had said. "Well," I thought, "I'm in one of those scattered places."

The early sprinkles were rather pleasant as I was fully warmed up from hiking fast. Sweat had dripped from under my hat, and the back of my shirt was damp in spite of the low humidity. "I can handle a scattered shower," I told myself. My spirits were still very high.

But the rain increased quickly. I began looking for an overhang to get out of the shower. Strong, gusty winds made it worse. I backed into a cleft in the rocks, only to get driven out by capricious winds that fairly focused the rain into my sanctuary. Still it poured. I was delighted! The rain would make some fantastic waterfalls that would spill into the gorge, and already, the storm was breaking up. Some good photos might be worth this whole extra hike.

Suddenly, I heard the clatter of falling rocks ahead of me on the trail. I stepped out into the rain for the sight of a lifetime. Perhaps a thousand feet (or maybe higher) above me, a massive rockslide was thundering down the near-vertical cliffs. Boulders the size of a school bus hit the cliff and leapt outward, some spinning violently like a pinwheel and hurling smaller pieces out. Some large boulders fairly exploded when they struck a solid bench on the cliffs. In spite of the rain, they made dust and sparks. It was spectacular! I was so mesmerized by the spectacle that I failed to see a few fragments heading my way. At least two chunks had some favorable bounces, and before I knew it, a black boulder about the size of a basketball smashed into the rocks about ten feet in front of me. I ducked back under my rain cover as a loaf-sized piece skipped over my shelter and rolled noisily into Bright Angel Creek.

I stayed under cover until the racket ceased. What a show it had been. I carefully peered out of my niche to make sure the slide had ended. As I started back up the trail, I could see that the rockslide had put a massive obstacle before me. Scanning the jumble of rock for a possible route over the mess, my eyes caught the sparkle of mica flakes or some other shiny crystals near the spot where the trail ended in the debris. I looked closer, noticing an apparent metallic luster as I moved in.

"Hmmmm . . . must be some bronze mica from altered Brahma Schist," I told myself with the cautious judgment of thirty years of geology. But a closer look told me what I still find very hard to believe. "It is metallic!" I said out loud. And in sing-song jubilance, I added, "and it don't look like pyyy-rrrite (pyrite)!"

The slab that blocked the trail had the remains of a slab of a quartz vein about eight feet long and as much as two feet high. It was up to half an inch thick. It looked as if someone had done sloppy trowel work with a poor grade of plaster and had smeared about five giant trowel loads on the rock face. Most of the "plaster" of white quartz included 20 percent to 50 percent gold. Some of it in tiny platelets, but some—especially the part that first caught my eye—was a thick sheet of pure gold.

I was afraid to get excited. It was the most dazzling thing I had ever seen. Better than those fantastic specimens I have seen in museums all around the West. This was a world-class gold specimen, no matter how you judge them. But it's in a national park. I couldn't legally even scratch it, let alone snitch a sample for my own pocket. And I'm so honest, my wife teases me about it. She likes to tell the story of how I wouldn't park under the NO PARKING sign in a ghost town in Nevada a few years back.

But I've never seen this much unguarded gold before. Could I scrape a few nuggets off with my knife then hurry back, not admitting that I had ever reached this part of Bright Angel Creek? Certainly the next guy on the trail would spot the gold. Odds are about one in three that the next guy will be a park ranger.

All the time I was convincing myself that I could not take a piece, my not-so-honest subconscious had taken my pocketknife out and was prying against an isolated piece of quartz that was riddled with gleaming yellow gold.

To my astonishment, the chunk popped out and fell on my shoe. When I bent down to pick it up, I saw several other small pieces of quartz—some with and some without gold. There were other pieces that had dropped off in the violence of the rockslide. "Good grief!" I gasped. "There could be a trail of gold clear up to the Tapeats Sandstone from this broken vein."

I found a thick slab of gneiss rock and quickly knocked off a double handful of "nuggets."

"I've already broken the law," I told myself. "Maybe I can clean it all off before somebody else gets here. And maybe it won't be a ranger."

The gold and quartz appeared to be half of a poorly cemented vein that had split wide open from the rockslide. I assumed the other half was somewhere up on the canyon wall. Perhaps it was still attached to the cliff, where nobody would ever climb. Certainly no one could ever mine it—at least, not without tons of equipment and a horribly dangerous cliff-hanging operation.

But I had work to do. My pockets were full: both hands were filled, and chunks were spilling along the trail as I searched for a place to hide my booty. If I could clean that whole face, I might get it all before somebody else finds it.

"Two hundred feet, that ought to be far enough, and above the trail where a fisherman won't stumble on to it." I was talking to myself, actually whispering for fear of being overheard. Trying to find a secure hole in all that solid bedrock was not easy. If a rock was loose, nature had already plucked it out and sent it tumbling into the creek.

I finally located a crack with a patch of cactus and a big scrawny yucca plant growing out of it. A dead, kinked flower stalk from the yucca made it look like the epitome of nonchalance. "A perfect hiding place," I thought.

Quickly I dumped my pockets and went back for more. It was four or five loads later, after I had emptied out my lunch to use the bread sack (which promptly broke with the heavy jagged chunks), when I realized I had a real problem. The shiny part of the vein—the part I had noticed in the very beginning—did not break off easily. I had broken my knife blade and had both hands bleeding from trying to remove the last square foot of gold. And it was the purest of the whole slab. I needed tools. And that flash of gold looked like a neon sign in the now bright sunlight.

Maybe I could cover it with mud and make it look like this boulder had slid over a patch of wet soil somewhere up above. Down by the creek, I found some soil. I pulled roots and mud and anything with which I could bind it all together. Luckily, I had chipped out enough gold to make a rough surface that the mud would cling to.

"But it won't withstand a rainstorm," I told myself. "I'd better get out with my cache. This secret is too obvious if it rains again."

After I had applied the mud, I looked at my watch and was startled to find it was four thirty. I would miss my steak dinner, and the others would be worried. I'd better go.

I cleaned up all the gold I could find. The rock slab showed some pretty strong mineral alteration, but even a good geologist would not expect what was under the mud. And he shouldn't have his trusty rock pick in the park either.

I paced the distance to my cache. It was about 175 feet. I picked out a couple of pounds of the high-grade stuff and tried to estimate the amount that remained. Easily fifty pounds. At least twenty pounds of that was GOLD—maybe even as much as thirty pounds!

I got back on the trail and brushed myself off. A few telltale flecks of gold were on my clothes, and my hands looked terrible. I cleaned up in the creek and concentrated on looking innocent.

I had to get my pocket-load out of the canyon before the gold was discovered, or I would be caught for sure. A few quick calculations in my mind (which was now about as calm as a turkey farm in a thunderstorm) told me that I had about $5,000 worth in my pockets and had a cache of about $100,000 in gold at $350 per ounce.

I skipped back to camp, humming and singing every lighthearted song I knew. I met no hikers, except a few strolling tourists who had ridden mules into Phantom Ranch.

Tomorrow morning, I would just hike on out of the Bright Angel Trail with my students as if nothing had happened. I wouldn't tell anyone. In a few weeks, I could go back and get my cache under the yucca stalk.

In camp, I apologized to my students for missing my $16.50 steak with them, and I made an excuse about hiking up a side canyon and having trouble finding a safe route back down. Nobody seemed to care anyway.

In the campground, however, a new twist developed. Alongside the campground trails, which are neatly marked with parallel rows of stones, are rustic memorabilia of old Phantom Ranch. There was a small wagon wheel, part of an old water pump, and the remains of a horse-drawn plow. The single remaining plow blade was attached to a heavy iron boom of some sort, with most of the wooden-handle parts rotted away. I scuffed the rusted plow blade with a rock and found that it was still good, solid steel. The shape was about right with the remaining iron to use it like a short-handled hoe or adze.

When it got dark, I lugged the heavy plow parts down to the Colorado River and waited in the brush by Bright Angel Creek until the last campers abandoned the big sandbar. It was midnight before the place was vacant. I had a plan to break off about twenty unnecessary pounds of the plow. Using an assortment of boulders and with a lot of twisting and prying, I finally broke the boom so that about fifteen pounds of custom "gold chisel" remained.

At camp, I scrawled a note that read, "Have climbed up the Clear Creek trail to watch the sunrise. See you at Indian Gardens." I tied the note to my tent flap and picked up some food plus the stuff-bag for my sleeping bag and the little bag for my tent. About three a.m., I started out for my gold mine. It was tough walking by starlight, but the trail was fairly smooth. I figured a park ranger would make an early-morning patrol between Cottonwood and Phantom Ranch. I had to remove my gold before the ranger got there.

About half a mile short of my treasure, it was light enough to see. "Perfect timing," I figured, but I was practically exhausted. I still had to lug my camp gear five miles up to our last camp at Indian Gardens before the day was over.

The plow-chisel was perfect. It made a clanking sound that I was afraid might be heard on the South Rim, but it neatly stripped the ore from the altered contact rock.

By six a.m., the face was clean. I had about ten pounds of rocks in my bag—about 80 percent gold. Not bad for a day's work! I began to relax a bit. I cleaned all the chips off the ground and checked to see what else had fallen off the slab as it rolled to rest. A few more chunks were down by the stream. Some pieces had even fallen below the big slab. That seemed strange, but I carefully cleaned it all up. But there was more even down to the creek. I had to get it all to avoid any careful snooping. I went down to the creek. Still more gold. Time was running out! If I could just be hiking on the trail, I could be casual when the rangers came. If I was groveling about with my hands and pockets full of gold, I would be in trouble.

Finally, I had the place tidy. At least, no *obvious* gold remained. I climbed up on the boulder that had lodged on the creek. From this high position, I could see the scale of the big rockslide. It was impressive. Like a tall building had collapsed by the creek.

I peered over the edge and looked down in the new pool of water that the slide made. The old fisherman in me just had to check to see if this new obstruction in the creek had brought any trout into it. Oh no! Not fish but the boulder I stood on was apparently the matching piece of the slab that blocked the trail. Right at the water level was a bright discontinuous quartz vein, loaded with gold. The first fisherman on the stream would find this slab of gold.

It was 8:30 a.m. Surely a ranger was near. I tossed my plow-chisel in the creek and wrestled some boulders into the stream until I had a pile to cover the face of the gold. A few more for good measure and back to my yucca plant to fill my gold bags. About twenty feet short of my cache, I heard a boot grind some rocks on the trail; and a young, thin park ranger came into view, about two hundred yards away. I dropped back onto the trail and examined a cluster of small flowers as he approached.

"Wow," he said. "What happened here?" He had neat dark hair, but his name tag said *O'Keefe*. With a name like that, I would expect to see a redhead.

"Must have been a dandy rockslide," I said. Then, after a pause, I asked him, "How much farther to Ribbon Falls?"

"Oh, it's another two and a half—maybe three—miles," he said.

"Is it worth the hike?" I asked, trying to divert his attention from the slide. (I had seen the falls on a previous trip.)

The ranger gave me a quick rundown on Ribbon Falls, but his mind was on the slide. He snooped around where the trail was blocked. I was sure he would find where my gold was chipped away.

"How long you been here?" he asked.

"Oh . . . about fifteen minutes," I lied. It really hurt my conscience to lie. I guess one sneaky move sets a pattern for more. First I stole the gold, then I wrecked the old plow in camp, and now I'm lying to cover my actions. Gold has already changed me.

The ranger scampered over the slide and climbed up to a rocky point across the creek. He paused a moment to look into the new fishing hole where I had buried the old plow. My time was fading fast. I still had three or four miles to hike back to camp and then load up my pack for a five-mile climb up to Indian Gardens. And I was tired enough to sleep on a cactus.

The ranger was talking on his radio. Had he caught me already? I strolled closer. From the few words I heard, I decided he was calling for a work crew to open the trail. He came back and visited for a while then casually wished he had some lunch because he was planning to wait for the work crew.

I had run out of choices. I couldn't grab any of my cache with a ranger there, and I needed to get to my camp moved on up to Indian Gardens. Most of all, I needed some sleep. I said a weak good-bye to the ranger and headed back to camp. I had about two pounds of samples in my pockets from the slab in the creek, plus the ten from the chise operation in my stuff-bag. My wages for the day came to about $50,0 I figured. And it was only nine fifteen!

My walk back to camp was laborious. I stumbled several tir fatigue, but my face had a wry grin glued on permanently. B I had my pack loaded, and I munched my last two cand passed the mule stables and trudged across the pipe b to Indian Gardens.

When I got to the garden camp, my left ankle pained me so much with every step that I was lurching along the trail like a villain from a horror movie. I limped heavily on the right knee, which began to throb. I was a mess. I didn't try to hide it from my students. What should have been a three-hour hike had taken me five hours. Tomorrow, the climb to the rim would be worse. With very few pleasantries with my students, I apologized for being so old and decrepit and laid my pad and sleeping bag out on the ground and died. No tent, no supper—just sleep!

The tunnel near the top of the Bright Angel Trail
on the South Rim of the Grand Canyon.

Somehow I got out of the canyon. I was dreadfully slow, and the extra weight of the gold in my pack made it feel like a hundred pounds instead of the thirty-six pounds I had started with. When I staggered through the little rock arch just below the top, I had a funny thought that the park service might have hidden a metal detector in the arch, like we see at airports, to check my pack for extra metal.

When I got home, I told no one about my gold. I stashed it under some rocks in a bucket in my garage. My plan was to go back to my cache as soon as possible, or maybe next spring with my usual Grand Canyon class. When I had all the gold home, I would buy into an abandoned gold claim and unload my gold over a period of time as a new development on an old claim.

The rest of the year went by slowly. The days I could get loose, I could not get a campsite permit. Even permits to hike the canyon with my spring class would only allow one night on the bottom and two nights at Indian Gardens. That would complicate my project, but it could still be done. I had already proved to myself that I could hike to the slide and pack out to Indian Gardens in one day. But not with fifty pounds of high-grade gold ore!

In December, I started workouts with a heavy pack. I hiked briskly around a nearby park with fifty pounds of sugar in my pack. It was grueling but the only way I knew to have full control of the gold. Whenever I could, I'd lug the pack full of sugar up and down my basement stairs. I could do 150 round-trips without stopping by the time the spring field trip came. I felt I was ready.

When the class started down the South Kaibab Trail, my pack was a bare-boned twenty-seven pounds. With the gold from my cache, it would go over seventy pounds. I figured that I could pay a few bucks and send most of my camp gear out on a mule. Then I could use the pack frame to haul only gold. I'd have my four-pound sleeping bag and a pound of trail mix to eat. I was counting on extra food from the students.

The class had the usual problems with trail trauma. The bar stop at the Phantom Ranch canteen seemed to go on forever. I was lousy company for my class, but I was thinking about my fifty-pound cache of gold about four miles away.

I don't think I ever went to sleep. I tossed and turned all night. My eyelids were virtually locked in the open position. At four a.m., I wrote another note for my tent flap: "Have gone up the side to watch the sunrise. Back at 10:00 a.m."

Again, I stumbled up the trail with only starlight. Somehow it was harder than last year—and this time, I was not carrying an old plow blade. Daylight caught me approaching the slide. It was mostly as I had left it, except for some freshly broken rocks and a fairly good trail built through and over the slide. It looked like they used a lot of powder to make the new trail.

I climbed the highest boulder and checked the trail beyond—just in case some early hiker or a pesky ranger was making his rounds. There was no one. Sunrise was still half an hour away, and it would not reach the bottom for several more hours. In the silence, the canyon was magnificent. This early, most of the cliffs were somber grays and bluish-grays. The canyon seemed even deeper in poor light.

Convinced I was alone, I turned toward the cache. I felt my heart start to pound—even more than from the brisk walk. I only counted fifty feet before I could see the patch of cactus and my yucca plant. The kinked flower stalk was gone, but I recognized my old yucca friend.

"How's our treasure?" I whispered as I got close enough. "Do you know you are the wealthiest yucca in the world?"

I grabbed the loose slab that covered my gold and laid it aside, trying to make as little noise as possible, even though there was probably nobody closer than three miles.

"It's gone! Damn!" I looked carefully at the hole. It was just as I remembered it before I filled it with gold. Whoever got the gold didn't leave a single flake.

As I returned to Phantom Ranch, the Grand Canyon did not seem so grand anymore. I couldn't complain because it was all stolen gold in the first place. What a sad turn in my life. "But, old man," I told myself, "you did get away with part of it." It was sort of a "perfect crime." I walked back to my tent with a blank mind and a blank stare.

As I finished packing my gear, a young, slim, dark-haired ranger passed through the empty adjacent camp. He stooped to pick up a bit of gum wrapper or some sort of small litter. I stared at him. He dropped the paper thing into a small plastic bag and looked right at me, apparently sensing my stare.

"Good morning," he said. "Is everything okay?" He started toward me. I strained to see his name tag. He was puzzled by my behavior and came closer.

"Morgan," I said quietly to myself. "It's not O'Keefe."

"Pardon me," he said. "I couldn't hear you."

"I thought for a minute that you were O'Keefe."

"No, O'Keefe quit last summer. Guess he had a rich aunt in Montana that died and left him a bunch of money."

"Oh," I said, and slung a measly twenty-seven-pound pack on my back. "Some people have all the luck."

THE PLACER GOLD PROJECT

Mesa State College offered a six-credit-hour summer camp for geology majors. It involved several days near the campus measuring and describing rock formations near Grand Junction in the Colorado National Monument. More days were spent in nearby Unaweep Canyon, and other weeks in varied geologic situations in western Colorado. We had three teachers, and we split up the assignments so that two of the faculty would be with the students each week.

One of our favorite projects was to have the class camp on Sheephorn Creek, near the small railroad siding at Radium, Colorado. From Radium, the trains work their way up the Colorado River into Gore Canyon en route to the Continental Divide and the Moffat Tunnel before dropping down on the east side of the Rockies. The area is very scenic and has some complicated geology. When we did the field camp there, only one obscure report of the local geology had been published, and we faculty checked it out of the library so the students would not be able to find it. We would assign a couple of square miles of terrain to each pair of students and let them do some serious field work to map their particular piece of the country. One additional little project that I controlled was to have the students calculate the amount of placer gold that was contained in a large gravel terrace on the south side of the river three miles east of Radium. An old placer operation had left a small pit in the gravel, and I would pan some of the gravel to show them that there really was some gold in the gravel terrace. I assigned each pair of students a spot to take a representative sample of the gravel in a five-gallon bucket. The students would calculate the volume of gravel in the buckets, and then I would pan the gold out of each bucket and report the amount of gold contained in each sample. The students would have to measure the approximate thickness and area of the gravel, and then apply the volume of gold per cubic yard based on the values from the sampling.

Most of the work was done by me because I would pan all the buckets of gravel and weigh the small amount of gold from each sample on a sensitive electronic balance to give them data points on the gravel terrace. I enjoyed all the gold panning, and it gave me something to do while the students were mapping their assigned sections. I did all the panning because I have had a lot of practice working with the very fine grains we were dealing with. Big "colors" might be 0.5 mm. Most of the stuff was smaller than 0.05 mm. The biggest piece I found in the first two years I assigned the project was a little smaller than the head of a wooden match. One grain like that would weigh more than all the gold in most individual buckets. I gave each student the gold from his/her bucket in a little glass vial. They could treasure it for life if they chose.

The results of the assignment were interesting. Some students had trouble calculating the volume of a partly filled five-gallon bucket. Estimates of the thickness of the deposit were not very consistent, and my measurements of the amount of gold in each sample were reported in grams, and they had to calculate the value in ounces per cubic yard.

Most of them did reach the proper conclusion. The correct answer boiled down to the fact that the value of gold in the terrace was not worth the cost of recovering the gold at the current price of gold. The total value changed each year because the value of gold changed each year.

In about 1990, Dr. Verner Johnson and I were in charge of the field camp on the day we did the placer gold project. Verner was probably the hardest working and most conscientious of our geology faculty. His credentials are in geophysics, and he has a hearing impairment that makes him a little hard to understand when you first meet him. I think he works harder to compensate for the problem, and most of us appreciate the extra effort on his part. If he can see your face when you talk to him, he is very good. If he is not looking at you, sometimes there is no conversation. When I took him and the students to my favorite old placer pit, I collected some gravel and passed out a gold pan to Verner and each of the students as I started my usual explanation of "how to pan gold." After a few demonstrations, the students began to get the hang of the basics. Verner took a pan full of gravel and pitched in with the rest of the class.

I collected some gravel from a variety of sites in the old placer pit, the same as other years. From high on the upstream edge of the terrace, among the roots of a gnarled pine tree, I got a full panload of pretty coarse gravel and the included sand matrix. Using a half-inch plastic grating, I shook away all the pebbles and cobbles and then dumped the fines through a ¼-inch screen into another pan. I took that down to the edge of the water and began the dipping and shaking to concentrate the heavy black sand. All the while, I kept explaining what I was doing and why. Several students were watching each step of the procedure because most of them had never actually watched someone pan for gold. About the time I was getting ready to swirl the water over my concentrate to see if there were any tiny flakes present, I saw a couple of little nuggets that broke free from the black sand. I was so startled that I slipped my footing on some moss-covered rocks underfoot and almost dropped the pan.

"Whoa, what have we here!" I squeaked. I had never seen grains that large on the Colorado River. I quickly finished that panload and found the normal small colors, and a third small nugget to join the first two. Wow! This was exciting.

Verner noticed the commotion among the students and came over to where I was working. His eyes brightened instantly when he saw the size of the three grains. He finished the pan he was working on and headed back to the gnarly pine where I had taken my sample. He quickly had another panload of stuff heading to the edge of the river. I also went back to the gnarly pine to get another panload, thinking that I had found a particularly rich spot on the old gravel terrace. Of course, I was explaining to the students how capricious the gold in a gravel deposit can be. I was obviously much more agitated because I really thought I had found a better place to get a panload of gravel. I worked down the material to the black sand, and there were no more little nuggets. I did a third panload and still no more little nuggets. Finally, I looked up to my attentive students and said accusingly, "All right, who salted my gold pan with those little nuggets?"

I knew that one student, Frank Russell, had a gold claim in the San Juan Mountains, and he may own a little gold. Another student, Dave Wolny, was mischievous enough to pull a prank on a professor. Somehow someone had sneaked the nuggets into my first pan while I was explaining the procedure. I looked straight at Dave Wolny, but he didn't look very guilty. Bill Conner also looked pretty innocent, but soon they began to waver, and finally they admitted the prank. The nuggets were Frank's. They feared for their grade in the field camp. That was a pretty dirty trick to pull on an unsuspecting old prof.

Instead of punishing them, I complimented them for doing such a slick job of salting my sample. It became an object lesson for the students on how easy it is to alter the value of a prospective gold deposit by salting a sample with gold.

All the discussion about salting my demonstration pan was missed by the other teacher, Professor Verner Johnson, because he has a hearing impairment. All he understood was that I got three nice little nuggets on the first pan that I worked down to the black sand for the students. He was still sloshing sand down on the riverbank, hoping to get his own collection of little gold nuggets. It was a long time before Verner understood what happened down there on the riverbank, and I don't think he was very amused by the prank. I thought it was a great stunt, although it made me look pretty silly for a while. If I hadn't panned hundreds of samples along the Colorado River in the writing of my little pamphlet "Where is the gold on the Colorado River," I may have been puzzled for a lot longer. I actually had found a huge reserve of placer gold, but it was scattered along the Colorado River for hundreds of miles and was rarely concentrated enough to make a commercial deposit.

Treasure Number 11

WRITE A BOOK

This little booklet quickly sold out during the fluctuations of the price of gold in the 1980s. The second printing also lasted only a short time.

In 1982, my obsession with gold led me to publish a little 5×9-inch booklet titled "Where's the Gold on the Colorado River—and how do you get it out?" It had only fifty-two pages, but it included some color photomicrographs of tiny gold flakes less than a millimeter in size. They look pretty impressive if you don't care about size. Other pages tell how the gold gets into the rivers and how to pan the gold out of the river sediments. Some sketches and black-and-white photos help explain the procedure. The index tells how much gold I recovered in 217 panloads of sediment taken along the course of the Colorado River. Samples start near Granby, Colorado, and end near Moab, Utah—plus one sample at Phantom Ranch in the Grand Canyon. There is gold farther downstream, but not much. In fact, there is not much anywhere on the Colorado compared with many other Western streams.

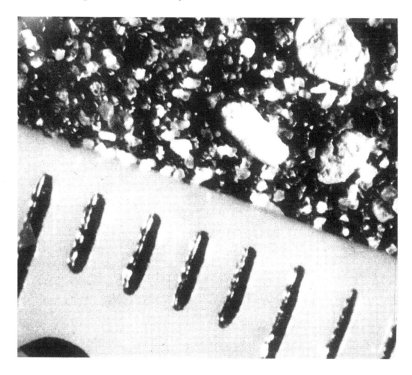

Three grains of gold, two that are flattened from a long journey down the Colorado River in Colorado. The third grain, in the lower right, is angular and was collected in a creek near the source of the gold near Virginia City, Nevada, in the 1980s. The scale is in millimeters.

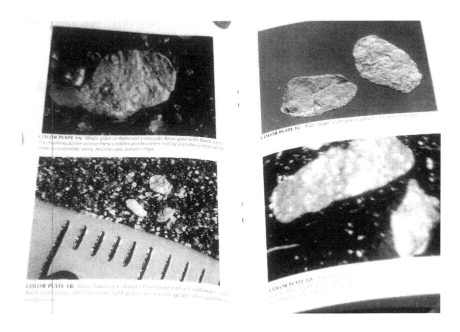

COLOR PLATE 1A: Single grain of flattened Colorado River gold with black spot. The crushing action pulverizes cobbles and boulders rolling with the gold grains them to resemble tiny, microscopic potato chips.

COLOR PLATE 1C: Two "large" gold grains about

COLOR PLATE 1B: Two flakes of Colorado River gold with a 1 million Black Gold grains are indicative light grains are mostly quartz. Red comparison.

COLOR PLATE 1D:

This is the centerfold of the booklet "Where Is the Gold on the Colorado River?"

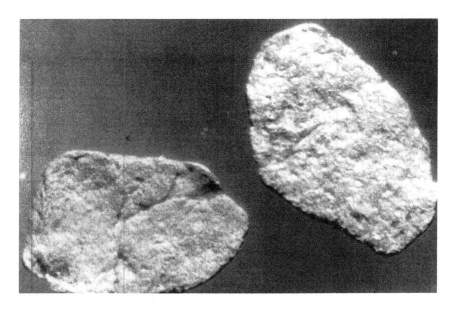

Two flattened pieces of gold from the Colorado River. Each is about 1.0 mm in size and has travelled more than a hundred miles downstream with the sand and gravel of the streambed.

Publishing my little gold pamphlet made a rather puny treasure. I paid about $3 a copy to get it in print and sold them for only $3.25 each. However, when the price of gold climbed to $1,000 an ounce, the little book sold like hotcakes. The second printing, using the original plates, cost about half as much; and the selling price did not change. Aha! I was making a pretty good profit. Not what you would call a big treasure, but the process has some merit. Maybe my "gold" treasure might be in writing. If the pen is mightier than the sword, why not apply it to a fortune in gold!

Soon the price of gold fell and sales of the little book dwindled, so I chose not to do a third printing. Perhaps that was a bad decision because in 2009 I learned that on the Internet one book had sold for $17 and another for $43.

Treasure Number 12

MAYBE WRITE A BIGGER BOOK

The work at Mesa State College in Grand Junction included a course titled "Geology of Colorado." Not willing to give up on the search for treasure in the rocks, I wrangled a semester of sabbatical leave to write a text and take photos for my course. It would be a basic geology book, but virtually all the examples of the basics would be in Colorado. All I was lacking for all phases of geology was an ocean; but historically, Colorado has had oceans more often than not. I used two cameras with two kinds of film. One set of prints were black-and-white for a cheap text for my students, and the other set was color shots for a deluxe version of the same book for tourists and people with some extra money.

This 8.5×11-inch paperback in black-and-white
(except the cover) did nine thousand copies.

And I became your geologist!

Starting in 1994, the first five thousand copies of the cheap version sold well. My geology course was popular (partly because the text was cheap), and my required text went quickly. I did a second printing of another four thousand, and it sold well too—until my knees, ankles, and mind began to fail, and I stopped teaching in 2000. Without the demand from my class, the sales slipped. Better books with color photos replaced mine, but a few orders were still coming in 2013. Sales will probably end about the time the inventory is gone. In nineteen years, the book made nearly as much for me as a year's teaching salary. I never published the deluxe edition, and I never made a fortune with the book. Once at a convention of geologists in Durango, Colorado, one of my associates introduced me to a group of his friends and he said, "Foutz is published too, and he made money off his book!"

Most books written by stuffy professors don't get a lot of readership. Also on the bright side, I didn't pay for an expensive version and get stuck with a room full of books with no market.

TREASURE NUMBER 13

FISHING AT LEE'S FERRY

On my way to a long-awaited fishing trip on the Colorado River below Lake Powell, I stopped in at a sports shop in Page, Utah, to get a three-day fishing license. I was a little ahead of schedule, so I also browsed the Blair Trading Post and John Wesley Powell Museum. With some french fries and a big milk shake from the mini McDonald's at the south end of town, I pushed on down the scorching road for Lee's Ferry. Still early for my appointed time to start fishing, I wandered around among the homes and the old homestead at the "Lonesome Dell Ranch." From my cursory visit to the Glen Canyon area, I gleaned some stimulating information.

Allegedly, John D. Lee was run out of southern Utah because of his connection with the Mountain Meadows Massacre. In that incident, some renegade Mormons attacked a wagon train of Arkansas and Missouri travelers in the 1870s and killed a number of people. John Lee built a ferryboat at one of the few sites where the Colorado River could be crossed between the Grand Canyon and Moab, Utah. The place became known as Lee's Ferry. While at Lee's Ferry, some amount of gold was reported in the brightly colored shales of the Chinle Formation. The prospected shale outcrop is exposed as a simple pit near Lee's farm and can be seen by anyone near the river crossing. The lore of the area, according to a tour guide at Page, Arizona, is that the metal rhodium is compounded with the fine "flake" gold, and it makes the separation difficult and costly. At first, Lee tried to smelt the clay by using wood fires, and finally coal was hauled in from Warm Creek, about fifteen miles upstream. A mule trail to the coal veins is still visible, where it was chiseled out of massive sandstone cliffs that tower over the old homestead. He even built a steam-powered boat and tried to tow a barge to the coal deposit, and then carry heavy loads of coal down to the ferry to smelt the gold ore. The operation never made any money, and the project was abandoned after only a few runs for coal. No record of any gold sales is available today. Part of the old boat lies submerged near the bank on the west side of the river as if it had sunk while tied up at a dock.

In the stifling midday sun, I eased myself down to the prickly soil, looking for a place to sit without risking too much pain and blood. Plants are rare on soil near the parking area, but each of them has a pricking device. I tossed out the obvious sharp twigs and spikes and sprawled out on the riverbank. In the hot, dead air, I squinted up against the sun and could make out a few switchbacks on the old mule trail. It must have been a miserable descent on the precarious trail leading off the flat rim of red sandstone down to the ferry and Lee's farm. Where the trail twists back and forth over the bare sandstone, the mule trains must have clattered occasionally when they kicked pebbles over the side, or when shod hooves nicked the bedrock. A slip might cause a tumble of 1,500 feet to the bottom. Clay and sand from the soft shale were probably used to soften the trail for animal hooves or hiker's boots.

As I pondered how tough it must have been to live here in the 1870s, a thought sneaked into my mind. "Gold in the Chinle Shale. Huh. That's a bit odd." I would have guessed it would be in the gravel just under the Chinle. Hmmm . . . there is a pit in the white clays near the base of the Chinle, but a fossil placer deposit in the gravel makes a lot more sense to me. They say the bright clays of the Chinle include a lot of volcanic ash; but if it contains gold, it would be every place the Chinle occurs, maybe covering the whole Painted Desert. I would buy the idea of an isolated vein that was dismantled by erosion and transported by streams back in early Chinle time; then it could make a high-grade placer. But that is not the story in the local tourist pamphlets.

I tossed a small pebble toward the outline of the old steamboat lying submerged below me. The hulk shimmered under three or four feet of icy water which emerged from the turbines below Glen Canyon Dam about ten miles upstream from Lee's Ferry.

"Maybe there is a nice fat rainbow trout by that old wreck," I said to myself as I leaned a little closer to look at the shadows alongside the boat.

There was a little glare from the river, as a perfectly cloudless sky peered back at me from the surface of the water. Some small willows (actually tamarisks) squirmed under a gentle flow from the stream; but except for a faint gurgle from some rocks against the bank, all was breathlessly silent. Even the bugs were quiet. I saw no fish. Straining my ears, I tried to hear the sound of the mild rapids a few hundred yards downstream but could not hear them. There was a distant shout and a clank from the old ranch house where a few carloads of tourists were checking out the old spread. Finally, I heard the sound of a poorly muffled engine heading toward me from the old highway bridge.

"You're about due, Eric," I said to myself. "I can't fish until you bring me a pole."

Shortly, an old brown Bronco arrived with a family of tourists from New Mexico. Three chattering kids exploded on the otherwise silent parking area. The apparent mom and dad headed for the restrooms, and the kids scurried about the US Park Service displays.

Looking back at the river, I searched the banks to see if I could get to the water to fish. It was pretty steep, and the cobbles would be hard to stand on; but if the fishing was half as good as the reports say, it would be a simple job to fish.

"Did old John Lee get gold from the gravel along the river?" I was still chewing on the stories of gold at Lee's Ferry. There were no obvious pits in the gravel on either side of the river where serious gold dredging might have occurred. I know there is a little gold all along the Colorado because I have panned gold from some of its tributaries.

"Much of the gravel I am sitting on probably came from the Paria River, and it is probably barren of gold," I told myself. "Maybe they worked the gravel upstream around that bend—if they worked anything. I am not convinced."

Gold at Lee's Ferry did not fit. There are not very many gold prospects in the area, and certainly not any in the clays of the Chinle. Not even in the gravel below. Nevertheless, many pages of the local history mention a gold operation by Lee at this location.

Eric's dusty red pickup popped into view and startled the gold out of my mind, replacing it with rainbow trout sizzling in a BIG frying pan. Eric says the fish here are all over fifteen inches.

"Been here long?" he asked, squinting at me from under a soiled straw cowboy hat.

"'Bout half an hour," I lied, not admitting that I had driven too fast from Grand Junction and had been idling around for more than an hour. Our whole plan was to start fishing as soon as I could get here from my place. I had not been fishing since we split for college twenty years ago, and I was pretty excited. Eric worked for a wildlife group in Flagstaff that was trying to rebuild the eagle population in the southwest. He kept track of fish in Arizona, and he assured me this was "primo water."

"Did ya get your license?" he asked, with a tone in his voice that said he would be disgusted with me if I had neglected it.

"Yeah, at Page, like you suggested. Man, they really sock you for a three-day license for Arizona, don't they?"

"You'll get your money's worth, all three days," he said confidently. "Let's go make camp."

I walked back to my car as Eric wheeled the old truck around and headed for the campground. By the time I got to him, he had selected a site, unloaded some big bags from the truck, and was unpacking a huge blue nylon tent.

"Slide this into that." He pointed to a loop on the outside of the thing. "Now this in that."

"Are you expecting a scout troop or something?" I queried, noting the size of the tent.

"My good tent is too small for two, especially if you have to stay inside in the rain."

"Sure, rain," I said in disgust. "I'll bet they haven't seen rain here for a month."

"But when they do, it can wash you away," he came back, making sure that I knew that he was the Arizona outdoors expert.

We had the "camp" made almost instantly. A huge blue chateau in a mostly red desert. My first thought was of a big zit in the middle of Miss America's forehead. The thing was a screen shelter with the option of complete cover if it got cold, wet, or both. There was room enough for at least eight people. We had double pads and huge down sleeping bags, a stove, a fold-up table, folding chairs, a cooler with ice, drinks, food, and all the trimmings.

Eric wrapped his bag around the cooler, and we went back to the truck. "Now let's get down to business!" he said, rubbing his hands together and flashing a sinister sneer like the villain in a cheap movie.

Eric and I had planned for years to "get together for some river fishing, sometime," but with my new teaching job, we could never get time for it. I knew it was a bit of a sacrifice for him because he usually went with his wife and two sons.

A set of rapids starts at the campground, and the beautifully clear water looked increasingly like "primo water" to me.

Eric handed me a spinning rod complete with a split-shot sinker and a bucktail spinner that must have been left over from his last outing. Quickly, he rigged another with a Mepps lure with red stripes and a mini propeller that I had never seen before.

"I'm sorry that I don't have my own tackle," I said apologetically.

"Hey, man, you haven't been fishing for years."

"You're right." My voice was wistful. While I was getting along with my teaching, I was not living much. It has been a grind.

"You might want to put this on." He shoved a bundle of stuff at me. "It's a wet suit."

"We never used wet suits before." I was resisting the offer.

"We never tried to fish in water that just came from a lake five hundred feet deep." He was reminding me that the water just came from the bottom of Lake Powell.

"I'll go without for starters." The thought of a hot black suit in this scorching sun was an impossible idea.

"These are the first rapids in the Grand Canyon," Eric shouted over his shoulder as he began to edge his way into the riffle. "Sometimes they feed right here."

Eric was tall, skinny, and reddish-blond. His nearly orange hair hung out of his hat almost to his shoulders, with a kind of ratty frizz to it. His face was covered with big freckles, and his nose always had a scab from sunburn. Since I first saw him as a kid, he has had that scab on his nose. With a first name of Eric, his last name of Randall seemed to be a mismatch. He should have been an "Edvarsen" or something genuinely Scandinavian. He had sneakers on and the wet suit over his legs, but the top half of his wet suit rumpled about his waist.

His first cast was near perfect, hitting just beyond a submerged boulder, allowing him to drag his little Mepps spinner into the slow water behind the boulder. Nothing! He moved a couple of steps farther into the stream and cast again at the same spot. Again, nothing. I was thinking that it was not late enough in the day for the fish to bite, but he went ahead, sort of stumbling before he got a good place for each foot. If he should stumble, that half-donned wet suit might be real trouble for him; he might go right through the Grand Canyon. It was an ugly thought, but he was more than knee deep, and he must have had the same thought because he slipped his arms into the wet suit and zipped it closed

His third cast was for the same position behind a bigger underwater boulder nearly halfway across the river. He slowly started to retrieve the lure, allowing it to cross the middle of the eddy behind the boulder. Wham! He yanked the rod up, and immediately, a dandy rainbow flew up out of the hole and headed for Phoenix.

"Ha hahhhh!" he yelped as the fish whacked back into the water and headed downstream. I couldn't remember ever catching a fish that big.

Now my adrenaline was pumping, and I jammed myself into a higher gear and headed to the river about two hundred feet upstream from Eric. The water was slower at my place, and I stepped into the stream.

"Oops!" The water was much colder than I expected. It felt more like slush than plain water. The cold was numbing. "I'll get used to it," I promised myself.

My first three casts were not as productive as Eric's, and not nearly as accurate. I blamed it on unfamiliar equipment and a lack of recent practice. It was ten minutes before I had a strike, and I missed it. Eric had landed his first fish and was working away from me, farther downstream where the stream gets a little noisier. In a couple of hours, Eric came back to check on me. I had a twelve-incher, which seemed only half as big as the one Eric first hooked.

"What have you got?" he asked.

"This one is all." I meekly held up my catch. It was a fine pan fish, but a runt compared to the one he caught.

"We better get another one for supper."

"I am not that hungry. How many have you got?" I asked.

"I released mine," he said proudly. "We cannot keep many here, you know."

"Yeah, I know, but that first one was a beauty."

"If I kept them all, we would have to go home now. Come on down to my spot and we will get another one for dinner."

"Doggone," I mumbled to myself. "I hope I can do a lot better in 'his spot' or I will be mighty embarrassed with my poor fishing skills." Of course, my fishing was from the dry bank because the water was so cold, and I wouldn't use the wet suit.

"Let's trade poles in case that bucktail isn't good today." Eric was giving me every chance to catch fish.

I took his pole and waded out to knee-deep water and popped his little lure right where he suggested. As if Eric's trained fish was waiting for me, I instantly had a whopper on. I stumbled a bit on some loose cobbles on the bottom but managed to keep the rod tip high, and after a few long runs downstream, I had a beautiful fourteen-inch rainbow to hold up for Eric.

"Can you eat that one?" Eric asked.

"Not more than half of him," I said.

"Okay, we will share him. But we can come back before dark for some more fun—right?"

I was now impressed with Eric's primo water, and he sounded like it would only get better.

Back in the bright blue blight on the desert, we soon had the trout crackling in a black twelve-inch iron frying pan. The fish was too big, and even cut in half, it filled the pan completely. I began to feel that this was a perfect fishing trip. I would even use the wet suit on the next session as the air would be cooler in the evening.

Lounging on my sleeping bag with my feet propped up on the cooler, I felt the tension melt away from my shoulders, and the little shiver faded from my recent sortie in the icy water. Eric skillfully prepared the dinner of fish and fish and a side order of potato salad that his wife had sent along. Gazing up at our dazzling blue ceiling, the thought of John Lee's gold sneaked back into my mind.

"Do you know anything about the gold mine that was supposed to be around here back in the 1800s?"

"Not much. Old John Lee supposedly mined gold for a while, but it was never rich enough to make any money. Except for a rare place to cross the river, this site is not worth much unless you like to fish."

"Are there other gold mines in the area?" I persisted.

"Not that I know of."

"Well," I continued, "do you know of any mines in brightly colored shale?"

"Nope. But I am a biologist, not a miner. Now if eagles ate gold, I would know about it!" And he laughed as he plopped a ton of fish on my plate.

I've never tasted better fish. I have never enjoyed fishing as much as that afternoon. I was beginning to live anew. With the dinner finished and much of the stuff put away, Eric said, "We better get moving—there is not much daylight left."

I suggested that we go up by the old boat hull where the water was a bit quieter. He agreed and we took the truck to expedite the few hundred yards. With both of us in wet suits, we cautiously waded out. The bank was a lot steeper here. I was just above the old wreck, and he was upstream within talking range. Eric had switched to a fly rod, and I was back with the copper spinner with the fuzzy black bucktail. The sun had dropped below the horizon, and the deep reds and dark shadows made the blue sky look like a phony postcard. The colors were just too intense to be real. Before dark, Eric had hooked a couple of nice fish that got away, and I had landed one and released him. I don't know why I released him. I am basically a meat fisherman and usually keep all I get so that I won't have to go home without a full limit. Maybe that is a penalty I pay for fishing with a conservation biologist.

Just before dark, a really nice one rolled over near my lure just as I started to retrieve it by the boat hull. I cast again to bring it up alongside the hull. The fish came up again, but didn't take the lure. He was bigger than our dinner! One more try—a little deeper and a little slower on the retrieve.

"That's it," I said to the fish as he came for the lure. "Grab it!"

And he did just as I ordered. He came out of the water with a dozen shakes before he flopped back, sounding like a large beaver whacking his tail for a dive. He streaked back and forth over the old boat hull and then it was all over. The fish was gone, but I was still hooked on something on the old boat. I tugged this way and that a couple of times, but the hook stayed fast. I stepped out on the bank and, giving the line a little slack, I walked downstream from where I was hooked, hoping the hook would slip out of the snag. It was Eric's lure, and I hated to lose it.

"Hey, you really have a dandy," Eric said, finally showing some excitement with my fishing.

"Yeah, this one's a couple of tons. The fish scraped the hook off on the old boat."

I still could not get the lure free, and after so long, you just have to give it a tug and hope for the best. I tugged a bit, then harder, and finally a long steady pull until the line snapped. I got nothing back. I held the line up to show Eric.

"No problem," he said. "We have more stuff."

"Sorry," I said. The lure is rather incidental, but the time to change lures would mean going back to the truck and deciding what to try next. Fly fishing would be more fun, but Eric only had one fly rod. I looked back at the submerged boat where the spinner was lying on top of the boat, gleaming up at me. I edged into the water to see if I could reach down to the spinner, but it was too deep. Perhaps I could swim to it tomorrow if it was still there.

It was nearly dark, so I walked downstream to watch Eric. He was having little success, and when he saw me coming, he walked out of the water, and we quietly wriggled out of the wet suits. We were chilled, but the air temperature was at least 80 degrees, so the cold didn't last.

The evening sky was spectacular. The blue was bluer and the oranges were richer, and finally the blacks were blacker than I ever remembered. The few stars gradually brightened, and soon there were five times as many stars as I could see at home. Back in the big tent, we settled down for the night. We could hear a number of animals of the night outside. The place was fantastic in our big chateau with the screens down but all the flaps up.

In the morning, I had barely stirred when Eric said, "D'ya want fish for breakfast, or would you prefer bacon and eggs?"

"I can always have bacon and eggs. Let's go for"—I rubbed my hands and gave Eric a sinister sneer—"FISH!"

I had the first strike, but Eric caught breakfast. Again, it was delicious, and soon we were stuffed and back in business on the river. Within about five minutes, we both had a big fish hooked and they were tearing up and downstream, trying to tangle our lines. Eric was downstream, and I stumbled and flopped on the ground into a sitting position, then shuffled upstream to try to keep the lines clear. He released his, and I kept mine. After releasing two smaller rainbows, I worked my way back to the sunken boat. The copper spinner was still shimmering up to me in the morning sunlight. It was taunting me. Soon, I laid the pole on the bank, emptied my pockets, and zipped up my wet suit. I could get that lure.

"Yeeaaack, that is painfully cold," I shouted, as I ducked my head and had some water sneak in around my neck

"That thing is only worth two bucks," Eric shouted, trying to save me the plunge.

"It's the principle of the thing," I shouted back to him.

With a big gulp of air, I went down for the spinner. It was deeper than I had guessed (over six feet), and I missed the spinner with my first cool swipe. A second plunge would do it easily. I got down in a good position and found the lure with some line wrapped around a twisted chunk of rusty metal. When I pulled on it, a hook stabbed me in the base of my right thumb. In frustration and considerable pain, I grabbed the metal and the line and, with both hands, gave a hard pull. The lure and the line came off, and the metal ripped open a thin hole about a foot long in the boat before it tore out of my hand. Now I had a hook buried in one hand and a nasty gash in the thumb and first finger of the other—all for a two-dollar spinner. But I had seen something inside that thin hole.

By the time Eric was at my side, I had the hook out and was just letting my wounds bleed freely.

"Are you okay?" he asked anxiously.

"Aw, this is okay, but I saw something in that panel—and it was shiny."

As I debated whether to bandage the wounds or just let them go, we saw a Park Service pickup moving our way. He parked and the uniformed driver went to a display area and stuffed some pamphlets inside the container; and as he returned to his truck, he noticed us and probably saw some blood. He walked toward me.

"What happened?" he asked, with genuine concern for me.

"I snagged a lure on that old boat," I said, "and the boat bites."

"That's a bad cut, and that old hulk is pretty rusty. We should fix it up for you."

We walked over to his truck, and he took off his wide-brimmed hat to dig behind the seat. He was a good-looking, chunky Hispanic man about fifty years old with lots of gray in his curly hair. He had a permanent kindly smile. From a well-stocked first-aid kit, he put some almost-painless liquid on the wounds of the left hand and was going to stop when I put the right hand toward him, hinting, "This is the deep one where a hook got me."

He lightly probed the gash and said, looking for approval, "I should poke around on this one a little, and it will hurt."

"It already hurts," I said, forcing a chuckle.

He bandaged me quite skillfully, and I guessed that he had training for just this kind of incident. When he finished, he put away the first-aid kit and told me to keep an eye on the wounds to make sure they didn't get infected. I figured that all would be well and that I could go on fishing, although awkwardly.

When the ranger drove off, Eric was ready to finish the morning fishing. He headed downstream where the riffles started.

"I want to check that boat again," I told him.

"What in the world did you see back there?"

"I don't know," I told him, "but I am curious. There is some sort of box that has been welded on the top of that boat—and it has something in it."

It took a couple of plunges before I could bend the metal strip enough to get my fingers into the hole. When I touched the little shiny thing, I was able to work it through the hole, and I quickly brought it up to the surface. It was some sort of buckle made of brass that had been flapping in the current enough to get somewhat polished.

"What sort of treasure did you find?" Eric asked.

"It's a brass buckle, I think." I passed it to him to examine.

"Is there anything else in there?"

"I don't know. It was too dark to see inside." I glanced back toward the truck and asked, "Do you have any sort of crowbar or tool that I might use to pry open that flap of metal?"

He led me to the toolbox in the truck. There was a big screwdriver and an old rock pick with a striped leather handle.

"One of these ought to do the job," I said as I took the two tools toward Eric.

On the first try, the screwdriver slipped off the best leverage point, so I brought it up and traded Eric for the rock pick. With the pick, I was able to pry open a hole big enough to poke my hand in the hole. I surfaced and tossed Eric the pick and took a deep breath and went down to check the opening. It was a little spooky to put a bare hand into a dark hole. I wouldn't do it in the ocean, but nothing very dangerous should be in freshwater. I stuck my hand into the box and grabbed a fistful of heavy things and clutched them against my chest and sort of porpoised my way to the surface and to the bank. My reward was four links of very rusty chain, two pebbles, and a large bolt with a nut attached that was very rusty. The last item was a small heavy block. Eric called down to me that someone was coming. I was not concerned that someone was coming until I remembered that we were on Park Service property, and I should take only pictures and maybe a few fish.

A shiny new Cadillac from California pulled into the parking area, and four adults dressed for church stepped out to examine the tourist displays. Eric handed me my pole and nodded to a Park Service truck approaching. I dropped the junk in the rocks beside me and quickly cast my lure beyond the boat. With my sneaker, I scuffed some dry rocks over my little pile of junk and continued fishing. The rock hammer was already dry, so I left it in the open. The first-aid man had a partner this time, and the new man was interested in our fishing licenses. All was in order, and after asking me how the hands were, the two left in the Park Service truck. They didn't ask why I was all wet. Were they watching us from a rock someplace nearby? Do other fishermen dip all over to get cool in a hot wet suit? I was a little troubled, but felt that I had done no real wrong.

When the Cadillac left, I looked under the rocks at my booty. It was just junk—but rather exciting junk, inasmuch as it had been trapped in a sunken boat for over a hundred years. The little metal block had a shiny corner, and I picked it up and realized that it was VERY heavy. Some more noise and Eric nodded toward the road. More visitors! I unzipped the top of my wet suit and slipped the block into my shirt pocket as a vanload of river rafters came to check out the restrooms. Two more pickups loaded with gear for the same group came next. There were a dozen people there now, and just as they were starting to load up, Eric hooked a nice fish on his trusty Mepps lure.

The rafters watched Eric handle the fish. One of them even mentioned how artfully he did the job. It was a beauty! When he released the fish, there was a groan from the rafters, suggesting they had been fishing halfheartedly and had little to show for their efforts.

When the parking area cleared, I sneaked a look at my metal block. It had a little greenish film on it, but when I rubbed it on my shirt, it shined a bright GOLD! With my pole in my left and the block in the right hand, I worked my way out to where Eric was fishing. When I was close, I got Eric's attention and flashed the little block at him. His eyes nearly doubled in size. Even under the shade of his grimy hat, his blue eyes sparkled out at me.

"Let me see that again," he pleaded.

I sneaked my fingers open and tilted it toward the sun for more effect.

"Wow!"

With much thrashing of water, we ran to the bank and up to the level of the parking area. Leaning over the hood of the truck, we buffed the other faces and stared in amazement at the little block. It was about three inches long and about an inch thick. I had seen a ladle for casting gold "ingots" somewhere, but I never saw any gold from the ladles. There was some lettering that might have been stamped by some sort of tool die.

"Mrsvl 1871 .943," it read.

"Are there any more?" Eric asked.

"I don't know."

"How big is it?" he asked.

"I don't know," I answered again.

"How much does it weigh?" said Eric.

"I don't know," I said again.

"How much is it worth?" Eric was getting impatient.

"Hey, I don't know that either, but it's a lot," I said. "Yeah . . . a lot!"

Two cars with Arizona plates were entering the parking area. These newcomers were going fishing. Eric had one nice rainbow in the ice bag. He showed the new arrivals when they asked. They soon became focused on serious fishing, and Eric and I were almost forced to fish also. I fished by the old boat hull but didn't care if any fish were biting.

"Hey, fish, don't bother me just now. I have some serious thinking to do." That was a stupid thought to come into my head. I am a meat fisherman that is finally starting to live again, fishing in "primo water."

Eric shuffled down to the riffles, and we could not see each other until much later in the day. The Arizonans gradually worked away from the sunken boat, and I went back up to the chateau. Eric was already there, munching on some nuts and cookies and taking frequent chugs from a gallon jug of apple juice. Several other campers were nearby now, as the place was filling up for the weekend. We looked again at our little ingot.

"This thing weighs several ounces," Eric said, positively.

"And it's worth close to a thousand dollars," I added.

We went back to fishing the rest of the day, releasing several nice fish, but ending with a limit of the biggest. Neither of us could concentrate on the fish, however, because we each had a world-class case of "gold fever." It was getting worse as the day wore on. We knew we should replace the little ingot. We also knew that no other living person knew it was there. Were there any more? A tantalizing mystery. What was poured gold doing at Lee's Ferry?

"Eric," I began, hesitating a bit, "I don't remember any reports that Lee ever sold any gold." After an appropriate pause, I added, "And I think that this ingot was cast in Marysvale, not here. What was it doing welded in Lee's boat?"

"Where's Marysvale?" asked Eric.

"A couple of hundred miles north of here, near Richfield."

"Are there gold mines there?"

"There must be," I said. "I know there was a lot of uranium and other minerals taken out of there."

Eric narrowed his eyes at me. "Why not Marysville, California? That was a real gold camp."

"C'mon, Eric. Marysville is a thousand miles away."

"Right, and this is the only crossing on the Colorado River for hundreds of miles."

"Yes," I added, "and this gold might have been payment for a big group to cross the river on Lee's ferry. In the 1870s, it would be worth less than a hundred bucks. The old double-eagle dollars were only worth $20, and there were a lot of them in circulation."

Eric clasped his fingers behind his head and leaned back as far as the little camp chair would allow and, looking up at the darkening blue ceiling, mused, "I'd sure like to know the story this little ingot could tell."

I was aware that we had been away from the river a while, and posed a new question. "Do you suppose there's anybody out by the old hull now?"

Eric peeked out of the screen, looking in as many degrees as he could see. "I think most of the people are in camp. It's going to be dark pretty soon."

I grabbed my wet suit and headed out the screen door, urging, "We've just got time to check that boat before it gets too dark. There will be a lot more people around here tomorrow."

Eric was right behind me, and we were soon suited up and wading out to the boat. I faced him and whispered, "There is a sort of flat box about the size of a long briefcase welded to the top of whatever the whitish part of the boat is. The northeast base of it is ripped, and that's where I got the ingot. It has a ragged strip of metal on it, so be careful."

After a huge gulp of air, I went down, flailing my feet for a second or two with a noisy splash to keep from going away in the current. I reached the jagged flap too quickly, almost jabbing it into my nose; and while I held the metal to counteract the current, I groped into the hole with my free left hand. I barely had time to check a few objects before I had to come up for air. It had only been about ten seconds. I held up a large rusty nut.

"No luck," I reported. "You try it."

Eric did a slow jackknife into the water, but he also flailed a bit against the current until his feet went under. He was down there a long time, and I could hardly see what he was doing. The sky had some pale blue to the west, but most of the twilight was quickly fading. Eric spluttered to the surface, gasping for air. He held a cupped hand toward me, holding two blocky objects in it.

"Here's two more," he said casually, but his wide eyes gave him away. His straining lungs also verified his tremendous excitement.

"Your turn," he said, and down I went.

This dive was a lot smoother, and I had more time at the ripped box; but even with several swipes, I could only get a grip on one of the slippery blocks. Others clanked out of reach, and I tore a small hole in the elbow of my wet suit trying to stretch out farther into the hole.

"I got one more, but we need a stick," I announced. "About eighteen inches long with a knot or a crook at the end."

We waded downstream to some tamarisk that shivered in the current. I got out of the water long enough to get to my pocketknife and then waded to the shivering twigs. It was nearly dark now, and there were so many stars up in the sky that they might start to leak out. With my knife, I cut a shoot about half an inch thick and a couple of inches too long. The wood was wiry, and I planned to break it or at least bend it, to make a crook on the end. It broke, or kinked, at just the right angle. Eric was ready for the next dive, so I handed the stick to him while I struggled back into my suit.

Again, Eric was down a long time. He had rested a little while I was fixing the stick. When he came up, he had four blocks.

"I put some more out on top of the boat. There are still more in the box—wow!" he whispered.

I was facing the boat, and Eric was behind me. He passed me the stick, and with a little gurgle, I was out of sight, heading for the box. I scoured the box with the stick and brought out more of the little blocks and gathered a couple from the pile Eric had placed on top of the boat. When I came up, I had three clutched against my chest and was trying to swim with two more in my right hand. I think I was getting greedy.

Eric's next dive brought up five more, and he tossed the stick up on the bank.

"The last load is on the boat." He shivered and headed for the bank where we now had a nice little pile stashed.

I went down again and started up with six but dropped one back on top of the boat so that I wouldn't lose it trying to swim out. I passed my load to Eric and went back to get the last one. I even jammed the ripped panel shut with my sneaker as I kicked off to come back up.

Quickly we struggled out of the wet suits. We stuffed the treasure into the legs of the wet suits and headed back to camp. Walking back was exhilarating until we saw two pairs of headlights coming toward us.

"Oh no," I thought. "Have those rangers been watching us the whole time?" A horrible fright chilled me to the bone. "They couldn't know what we were doing—or could they?"

We put on a look of extreme innocence as we walked toward the headlights. I expected some spotlights to stab into the darkness and destroy our little fantasy. The cars slowed almost to a stop. We turned our heads to the side to avoid the glare of the lights and shuffled to the side and out of their way. The cars stopped, and a chubby face leaned out of the passenger window of the lead car.

"Is that the only camp around here?" he asked, beckoning with his head in the direction of our camp.

"That's it," Eric said.

"What a bummer!" came from inside the first car.

Eric and I heaved a big sigh of relief as the cars moved ahead to the parking area and turned around. We walked nonchalantly to our tent and went inside. For a moment, we considered packing up and leaving the area, but we felt secure that no one had any idea of what was in our tent. Eric closed the flaps on all the screens and dug a roll of paper towels out of our "kitchen." As we scrubbed the grime off our little blocks, we piled our treasure one gleaming brick at a time on top of my sleeping bag. We had twenty-five solid gold ingots—enough to build a nice little house on my sleeping bag. No two children ever enjoyed playing with blocks any more than we did in that ugly blue tent in the desert by the Colorado River.

"Okay, Eric," I said abruptly. "What is the secret of these gold bricks? Nobody ever paid this much for passage on Lee's ferry."

Eric stared a moment at the little brick in his hand, then faced me directly. "Suppose—and I have been stewing over this all evening— suppose somebody stole the gold in California and hid the gold on the boat." After a long pause, he added, "Lee might have been in on it or maybe not. There were a lot of pretty shifty characters around this area in those days."

"Hold on a second," I said. "We are assuming the gold was stolen. What if an honest gold shipment passed through here, and the carrier, expecting trouble, had Lee hold it for safekeeping?"

Eric cut in. "That story isn't exciting enough for this area. Here's the truth. There was a bank heist by a gang of famous desperadoes—maybe even pals of John Lee—and they brought the loot here. Lee hired them to help with the ferry and the farm, and they could draw from the gold as needed."

"Nope," I said. "If more than one person was involved, the gold would not be here now. Anybody could break into the boat if they knew there was a treasure there. It had to be Lee. He stole the gold, and then made a ruse of mining gold here so that he could melt the ingots down and pretend that he was smelting it from his own mine. When he died, he had to leave the gold in that strongbox. That accounts for the fact that nobody else could find more than a trace of gold around here."

We debated whether Lee was an honest man or a scoundrel until after midnight. Then, when our discussion had more yawns than complete sentences, we gave up and yielded to a most satisfying sleep.

Next morning, after the great blue monster was stuffed into its nest and all the gear was stowed in the proper place in the dirty red pickup, Eric eased the truck onto the road and began our exit. As we turned away from the pit in the white Chinle clay, Eric stopped and backed up about half a truck length for a better view of the "mine."

"There is the gold mine that had no gold," he said sadly.

"And under is the dark gravel that also had no gold," I added with even greater exaggerated sadness.

Then Eric rubbed his hands together with his familiar sneer and announced, "And in about two minutes, there will be a whole lot less gold around here than"—he chuckled—"than when there wasn't any!"

And I replied, "And that 'primo water' will never be the same again."

LOS TRES CABRAS

I finished high school with three great pals. We graduated in June 1950, and immediately, North Korea decided South Korea belonged to them, and they went about taking possession of South Korea. They may have had a few justifiable reasons for invading their neighbor, but to do it with tanks and heavy artillery was not very nice. In a very few days, the three of us could see that our lives would be deeply involved in the new "police action" in Korea. I remember on several days seeing huge B-36 bombers fly over our hometown, Ogden, Utah, heading west toward the Pacific Ocean and possibly Korea. A scant five years earlier, the first atomic bombs used in war were dropped on Japan, and we knew the B-36s could carry nuclear bombs to any point on the surface of the earth. One evening in that fateful June, we three young men gathered in Walt's car for a chat. It was Walt's father who owned the car—but to us it was Walt's car, just as my dad's car was mine and so on. Only one of us actually owned a car, and that was Eddy. I can't remember at the time if he had his Model A Ford, with a rumble seat in back, or his Hupmobile, which was a deluxe car but was old and had a cracked block in the engine and was cheap. Eddy was good with tools and could make it go.

It was after dark and Walt's car was in the garage, and a bare single light bulb hung down on a cord from the ceiling. We were not going to go anyplace, just talk in the car in the garage. The seats were comfortable; after all, it was a 1938 Packard. Our lives were at a crossroads, and we talked long into the night about our situation.

I had a small scholarship to attend Weber Junior College and was already enrolled to start in the fall. If a draft started, I might have an educational deferment until 1952 when I would graduate from Weber and be eligible for the draft. Jim and Eddy enlisted in the navy, and Walt either was drafted into the army or joined it and went to OCS (officer candidate school).

My brother Kent was drafted and went directly to Korea. He ended some of his letters with something like "Guys in the navy live first-class on those ships unless they are dying. Guys in the air force live first-class unless they are dying. We in the army don't know what first-class is, and we are dying—don't be in the infantry!" With Kent's advice, I went to Provo, Utah, in the spring of 1952 (just before graduation at Weber) and enlisted in the air force ROTC. I would have been drafted that summer, but I was in the air force. Walt went through OCS and spent his tour in ordinance and stayed in the U.S. all three years. Eddy did his three years in the navy. Jim chose the navy too, but he went into jet fighters and was lost over the Sea of Japan at night when he had a flameout and could not get a restart. They found no trace.

The three remaining pals—Walt, Eddy, and I—finished our service time and went on to successful careers; and in the 1990s, we all went to Colorado for a mining venture in the San Juan Mountains. Although Walt had moved to Moab, Utah, and Eddy was in Farmington, New Mexico, and my home was more than 200 miles from our chosen mine, we decided to try our luck. Mostly, we wanted to get out of the rat race and enjoy some quality time in the mountains. Because Lake Fork of the Gunnison River had hosted a lot of successful mining activity in the late 1800s and some mines were still active in 1990, we agreed to seek our fortunes near the small mountain town of Lake City.

Walt's career had been in business management, and Eddy was good at keeping mechanical things running. He also had advanced degrees in counseling. My work had been in geology, and they relied on me to find the good ore to make the venture succeed. It would be mostly luck if we were successful, but we knew we would enjoy a few years more of our lifelong friendship, and the mountain location would make even bad days better than the best that can be found in a city. Our wives and families were not nearly as enthusiastic as we men were, but we would not relocate them. They could stay in their comfortable homes, and we would take turns at the mine and even bring them together at

Lake City often enough for them to enjoy the mountains and the social relationships they had in common with us. Grandkids were another problem. We would work hard at giving them some exposure to our wonderful mountains and provide special outings with boating and fishing on Blue Mesa Reservoir and hunting in some of the best wildlife areas in the lower forty-eight states.

Lake San Cristobal is about four miles upstream from the town of Lake Fork on the Lake Fork of the Gunnison River. Los Tres Cabras would be about halfway up the timbered mountain on the right margin of the photograph. The bulge into the lake on the bottom of the photo is the remains of the Slumgullion earth flow, which began squishing into the lake about seven hundred years ago.

One gold mine was operating across the Lake Fork from the famous Slumgullion Slide, where a fairly recent (geologically) land failure had slowly rumbled and squished down thousands of feet on the north side of the river and actually pushed into the side of Lake San Cristobal. Glaciers had once scoured the valley and helped to make the scenery there rather spectacular. Many of Colorado's fifty-three "Fourteeners" (peaks over fourteen thousand feet) were in the San Juans; and many millions of dollars in gold, silver, copper, zinc, and lead had been recovered from the Lake Fork District.

I studied the county plats for many hours and used the US Geological Survey's geological quadrangle maps to select the most likely place for our mine. Most of the area had mining claims on top of other claims to put almost every acre within a mining claim. Six hundred or 1,300-foot claims are oriented to cover surface exposures of choice veins or hoped-for veins, and their corners overlap a lot because one prospector is covering what he wants but an adjacent miner with a standard-sized claim wants his to cover a different gully or outcrop. An abandoned mine only 1,100 feet from the mine that was operating in 1980 fit most of the criteria that I was looking for. It had a passable access road, fairly stable rock, and good timbers in the weak areas. Entry was nearly level for 600 feet, and several adits off the main bore followed some interesting brown gossan veinlets. A gossan is where sulfide minerals, including iron pyrite, have weathered (rusted); and some of the more valuable metals (if present) have leached out of the vein, leaving mostly iron rust. Lead, silver, zinc, and copper would leach away and descend in the groundwater to precipitate the metals near or in the water table. As the mountain erodes, or the water table fluctuates with climate, the minerals may be enriched several times over at depth.

The mine was the Joe Banner Mine, which was abandoned in 1904 after only a little production. Lead and zinc worth $4,000 had been shipped in 1902, and that was the only record of production I could find. There was no record of any gold or silver. Either the production was not profitable or the owner died or any number of problems caused the demise of the mine. I saw no evidence of cave-ins. The back (roof) had no roof bolts, yet the mine had clean walls and back with no gaping holes where blocks of rock had dropped out.

My pals agreed to reopen the mine. We would call it "Los Tres Cabras" because we were three old goats, and there are a lot of old Spanish names in the district. And Eddy was fluent in Spanish. We had been careful to drive our old commuter cars or my battered old Ford pickup whenever we visited the mine or stayed in Lake City. We rented a small shop on Bluff Street at the south end of town next to Fall Creek. We made sure that it had a tight roof and a good wood stove because we knew that winters at nearly nine thousand feet would be wicked. We planned to spend a lot of our time in the mine or in the shop, but there would be days (and even weeks) in the winter when we would not come to Lake City at all.

Our first order of business was security. I located a huge iron door among some junk at the old Hercules Powder Company near the mouth of Spanish Fork Canyon in Utah. It had been used on a storage vault probably back in the 1940s, and although very rusted, it was plenty sturdy and big enough for a large truck to pass through. With some major modifications, the door was installed at the mine entrance and fitted with a huge lock. "KEEP OUT" and "NO TRESPASSING" signs were posted along the tough barbed wire fence surrounding the entrance area. A serpentine roll of razor wire on top of the fence added a menacing touch. "HARD HAT AREA" adorned the big door.

Equipping the mine was a simple matter. Eddy had a former classmate friend who managed part of the scrap metal program at Geneva Steel in Provo, Utah. A few carloads of scrap came in on a train from northern Idaho, including some from the silver mining country near Kellogg, Idaho. There were pumps, ore cars, rails, jackhammers, and virtually tons of miscellaneous junk from a century of hard-rock mining in Idaho. The stuff was only worth the price of scrap, but it looked authentic. Eddy got a pair of drills and some rods and many pieces of equipment that looked like "tools of the trade" in hard-rock mining. Small broken rock bits were in the load, plus a few sledges and other hand tools. He had to pay for the stuff, but the price of scrap rises with other parts of the economy, and the supplies would remain at least as valuable as what Eddy paid for them. None of the hand tools had handles, so we had to buy handles and make them fit.

I visited a couple of coal mines near Grand Junction and was able to scrounge some worn-out work clothes and hard-toed boots. These were scattered around the outside of the heavy mine door, in clear view of anyone looking inside the fence. Some odd tool pieces were kept in the bed of my old Ford pickup, which eventually stayed at the mine or was used to commute from the shop in Lake City to the mine. We made sure there was room in the opening of the mine to park a pickup truck, and behind a grimy workbench, we built a pretty good "lunchroom"— which had a good ventilation fan with a big hose to the outside of the mine so that the room would not get too stuffy. We had a refrigerator and a small wood-burning stove that was also piped to the outside of the mine. Central to the lunchroom was a table and chairs with good fluorescent lighting and a cabinet filled with playing cards, puzzles, games, and plenty of videos for the entertainment system. It was a fairly comfortable "den" for the workers—all three of us. There were enough chairs for ten people because we expected some family members to be there once in a while.

The shop in Lake City was the front room of a rustic "vintage" home. It was a solid home built after 1950, but it was done in unfinished logs and heavy timbers to look like part of the 1880s boom days of the historic mining center. The bathroom was the only part of the house that was not worthy of a modern dwelling, but Eddy had remodeled a couple of his own homes, and he jumped on a remake of the bathroom during our first week. In a month, he had a new tub and sink with state-of-the-art showerheads, taps, and the whole room in pale blue ceramic tile. All of it good enough for a four-star motel.

We isolated the big front room to make it a Spartan front office for a shoestring company. The wood floors were eight-inch-wide pine boards that had been covered with a shabby old carpet that we tore out. We found a cheap used table and an old rolltop desk with some damaged parts that we fixed with mismatched wood. We replaced the adequate lights with some bare 75-watt bulbs and added a neat new display case with fluorescent lights built in. I put a rusty sixteen-inch gold pan in as a display item with my total collection of small flakes of panned gold (about two grams) alongside a rock pick and a hand lens on a leather cord. It was a nice display but had nothing to do with hard-rock gold mining.

As our mine developed, I added appropriate ore samples of high-grade sulfide ore that contained impressive amounts of galena, sphalerite, and chalcopyrite (sulfides of lead, zinc, and copper respectively). A couple of small pieces with visible gold were finally added to the shelf with the gold pan where the light was best. The ore specimens cost me a little over $11 at a rock shop in Ouray, Colorado. The pieces with visible gold came from the curio shop at the Narrow Gauge Railroad station in Silverton. They were pretty good specimens and cost $25.

After a few months, I borrowed a chunk of about forty pounds of high-grade ore that I had picked up on a field trip in the Idarado Mine at Red Mountain Pass south of Ouray. I had donated it to Mesa State College when I taught there. To get it out of the mine, I told my students that I needed a couple of "A" students to lug the thing out. Two volunteers quickly responded. It was a fine example of the hydrothermal replacement of sulfide ore in the Telluride Conglomerate. The mine geologist at the time was a Hispanic man from Fort Lewis College in Durango. He led us into the mine a couple of times back in the days when the company rules were a little more flexible for mine tours by college classes. The truth is that I don't think the Telluride Conglomerate is in the mines at Lake City; instead, the rock is all volcanic.

The "shop" had no function other than a dwelling for us when we were at Lake City and working in the mine. We had a small shingle over the front porch, but we didn't intend to do any business there. We did receive a little mail, but a lot of it was sent by us "miners" to our Los Tres Cabras Mine. Whenever we mailed anything, we made it a point to send it from Denver or Salt Lake City; and occasionally we would send something rather heavy, such as a rock or box of nails or a tool. Whenever one of us was in the shop, we left the door open and a few curious people dropped in. Most of them were tourists, but a few were locals just checking us out. Some of the men I recognized after we started eating at the local restaurants. Very few people asked about our mine, especially the first year, and we were very stingy with information. We generally told them that we weren't finding much.

In our first full summer of operation, we stayed pretty much to ourselves. We bought groceries and ate at the mine or at the office. Most of the time, only one of us was at the mine; and when we were there, we often brought our wife or some of the family. We toured the area a lot and enjoyed the mountains, but always in older cars. The pickup was kept behind the shop and was used to drive to the mine, as the road was not suitable for passenger cars. Kids could ride in the back of the truck, and the routine would be to drive to the gate, open the pair of locks on a heavy chain, and drive into the fenced area and lock the gate behind and then open the huge door and drive the truck into the mine. We usually closed the door behind the truck, and the rest of the visit would be in privacy. Sometimes we would leave the heavy mine door open, but most of our activity would be out of sight in the den, or deeper into the mine.

We usually took a few boxes of stuff into the mine and usually brought boxes of stuff out of the mine. We had a dozen or more sturdy old wooden fruit boxes from Talbot's fruit farms in Grand Junction.

We had a heavy metal cover over about a third of the bed in the truck, and we kept the boxes under the cover whenever we were moving to or from the mine. Several times a month, one of us would drive the truck back to my home in Grand Junction. We added more boxes on those trips and had a bigger cover for the whole bed of the truck. I spent a number of weeks alone at the mine in the fall of the first year. I spent time there in every month except January and February that first winter.

Our work in the second year started late in March, but we had to wait until mid-April before we could get a guy to plow our road open. After some busy weeks, I leased a big red Dodge Ram pickup; and in June, Walt drove to Lake City in his Cadillac. We began eating a few meals at Mammy's and the Tic Toc diner, and we always paid tips of at least 20 percent. The routine at the mine continued as before—take boxes in, bring boxes out, and occasionally leave the area with a truckload of boxes.

We didn't show at Lake City for the last two weeks of July, and in mid-August, Walt and I were in the shop when Eddy drove up in a new white Mercedes. We came out and talked with him on the curb for a while and then we went inside for most of the afternoon. Our red truck, a new Cadillac, and a white Mercedes remained parked along the street. The next day, we all went to the mine in the truck, and we stayed inside all day. When we came back to town, I left with a load of boxes in my truck, and Walt and Eddy followed me out of town in their cars.

Two days later, Eddy and I came back in the truck and had a busy day back at the mine. We left again in two days with another load. By the end of August, we had taken the big red truck away about six times, although the boxes were usually empty. In September, we made several more trips, and the boxes were still empty. In October, we did some hunting with the truck, and the stuff was all hunting gear, but the three of us did eat out all our meals in town. A week later, I brought my son for another hunting trip, then things slowed down and I only made a couple of appearances each month until April of the third year.

After we all got our taxes in, we arrived in time for dinner on the tenth of the month, and we chose to eat at the slightly more elegant Charlie P's. There are so few places to eat in Lake City that being more elegant is a marginal thing. We could have gone to the Western Belle, but it was part of a lodge and we were not staying there. At the shop, we parked the red truck, the Caddie, and the Mercedes on the street and stayed the night.

For a week, we had breakfast and dinner at Charlie P's and "worked" all day at the mine. We made sure to have clean clothes on for breakfast and grungy work clothes for dinner. Lunch, of course, was at the mine. We were in the third year now, having started with clunker cars and sack lunches and "working" a mine in a district where a lot of gold, silver, lead, zinc, copper, and other minerals have been recovered. We had moved up to new cars and a big new truck, and our lunches had gone from frugal stuff to the best in town, and we tipped well.

In early May, a skinny kid we knew from the gas station brought a couple of men up to us as we were leaving Charlie P's after dinner. The men wore suits, and the shorter one introduced himself as Sheldon Tanner, a financial planner from Denver. His partner was Whit Warner. Both men were about fifty, and they wanted to know about our mine. We invited them to follow us in the truck to our shop on Bluff Street where we pulled up chairs around our old table. Eddy brought out our new fluorescent light on a long flex pole that made our old table a workable conference table. Sheldon was an electrical engineer before he moved into the financial business, and he did most of the talking. I think Whit had a degree in business.

Most of the questions were aimed at me. Was I the retired geology teacher from Mesa State College, and what did I know about gold mining? I summarized some of my background, emphasizing the fact that most of my gold experience had been as a consultant on placer gold deposits. They wanted to know why we three were together, and we told them about our background back in the 1950s as neighborhood pals.

Sheldon and Whit were cordial. The questioning was gentle and not confrontational. We had a pleasant half hour before questions turned to what might be called "development" and "production" at our "gold mine."

Walt's people skills, developed over decades in retail management, took over a lot of the answers. "We don't really have a gold mine," he said. "It is more of a recreational outlet for us to enjoy retirement years together in a great location."

"What about all the truckloads of ore you've been taking out of here for the last couple of years?"

"We're not selling much of anything, but Dell here"—nodding toward me—"has been assembling some suites of weathered rock to give to some college teachers he knows for lab studies in geology."

"Isn't your mine the old Joe Banner mine?" asked Whit. He was looking over some notes in a small notebook.

"Yes," I said, "but it was shut down nearly a hundred years ago."

"Did it produce anything?" he asked.

Whit was looking sternly at me like he was trying to catch me in a lie. He had thick dark hair and dark brown eyes that were squinting a little at me, as if he was in bright sunlight.

"Not much that I could find in the county records," I said, shrugging a little.

"Was there any gold?" he continued.

"Not that I found any record of," I said.

He was getting more intense, and I was getting more casual. Both of them were quiet for a while.

"Have you found any gold in your new operations?"

Now it was Sheldon asking. His round face and very short, graying hair that was nearly gone on the top of his head and wire-rimmed round glasses reminded me somehow of an engraver. He peered at some of his own notes as if he had trouble seeing them clearly. Maybe he worked with large magnifying lenses over small print.

"We haven't recovered any gold," I said.

Whit sat up, a little bit more lively, asking, "But what about all the gold in that display over there with the gold pan?"

"Oh, that's placer gold that I have recovered from streams," I said.

"What streams?" Whit butted in, then he sat back a little as if he hadn't meant to be so challenging to me.

"All over—several states. That's my entire poke," I said.

Rather than be any more confrontational, our conversation relaxed. The two guests seemed satisfied that they had found out what they came for, and our conference ended. Everyone was cordial, and we told them they were welcome to come by again if they wished. They seemed to be disappointed in the meeting, but just as we were near the door to let them outside, Whit asked, "Can we visit the mine?"

The three of us stopped and hesitated a few awkward seconds. Finally, Walt said, "Well, there wouldn't be much point in that—it's not much to look at," implying that we were opposed to their examining the mine.

The two looked at each other, a little puzzled for a second or two, then continued out the door. We watched them pull their late-model Chevy sedan around and head back to the north. Before we went back inside, the Chevy stopped in a lighted area, and we noticed they had turned on the interior light in the car. We went inside, but we could see from a side window that they waited there possibly ten minutes before driving off.

The next morning as we were finishing breakfast at Charlie P's, Sheldon and Whit met us inside the restaurant. They were wearing more casual clothes, and each had a light jacket because it was rather chilly in the morning.

Sheldon spoke first, looking at me through the top of those round bifocal glasses. "What was that big rock you have as a doorstop in your shop—it seemed to contain a lot of shiny stuff?"

"Oh, that is a chunk of high-grade ore from a mine over by Ouray," I said.

"High grade of what?" Sheldon asked.

I wasn't sure how much technical talk he would understand, so I said, "Mostly zinc and lead. The bronze-looking stuff is chalcopyrite."

"What is chalcopyrite?" he asked.

"It is a copper and iron sulfide," I replied, noticing that he was quite curious about that boulder.

"Is there any gold in it?" he pressed me on.

"Probably some, but it would be pretty fine. I have not seen any that I was sure was gold," I said.

"Why do you have the rock?" he asked.

I probably sounded a little impatient with him and went through the whole story of finding it in the Idarado Mine and using it as a sample in our minerals lab at Mesa State College. He asked if he could see it again in daylight. It was a little awkward for a while, but I finally gave Eddy the keys to the truck, and he and Walt went on to the mine while I rode back to the shop with Sheldon and Whit. When we got inside, I left the door open so that the bright light from outside came through the door. The specimen is a lot more impressive in direct sunlight, so I picked it up and lugged it outside to the sunlight at the edge of the porch. It was a bit of a struggle because the thing weighed about forty pounds.

"And this is not out of your mine?" Sheldon asked. I could tell he was not sure I was being truthful with him.

"No, these round pieces are pebbles of the Telluride Conglomerate, and you will notice that they are partly replaced around the edges with sulfide minerals."

"What was the name again of the mine this came from?" Now Whit was asking.

"The Idarado." And I hoisted the rock and took it back to the doorway.

Now Sheldon asked, "What kind of production did the Idarado have?"

I told them that the Idarado produced from several veins. And when the price of zinc was up, they mined a lot of zinc; and when copper was high, they could shift to more copper. Gold was present in most of the ore and quite rich in a few places. If gold prices were up, they would high-grade their mine for gold. Gold, silver, lead, zinc, and copper are present throughout the mine; but the richness of the veins varies a lot.

"How much money did the Idarado make?" Whit asked.

"Millions," I said, "and over a long time. It was still operating into the 1980s, I think."

By now, Sheldon had drifted over to my little display case, so I turned on the light in the case.

"Is this from your mine?" Sheldon asked, pointing to one of the display pieces.

"No," I said flatly.

"What about this one?" he asked as he pointed to one of the others.

"No, none of them are from our place."

Whit was looking closely at the samples with visible free gold. "What about these?"

"No," was my answer again. "These are from a rock shop in Ouray," I said, pointing at the shelf of mixed ore specimens.

"But what about these two," Whit said. "Is that gold?"

"Yes, that is gold—some pretty good pieces, in fact," I said, and Sheldon leaned close with Whit to look at the pieces. I moved to the back of the case and removed the two rocks with the free gold. They looked at them closely for at least half a minute. I took the hand lens from the other display and handed it to Sheldon. He obviously had not used a small hand lens much, so I showed him how to put the lens near the eye and then bring the sample closer until it came into focus. He fussed a bit until he got the light and the focus all worked out.

"Hmmm . . ." was all he could come up with, and Whit was eagerly anticipating his turn to look at the gold with a lens.

When Whit finally got the light and the lens adjusted and in focus, he said a soft "Oooo—wow!"

"Where did these come from?" asked Sheldon.

I paused a while, trying to remember for sure where I had bought them. "Ah . . . I got them at the curio shop in the Narrow Gauge Railway station at Silverton."

"And what did you have to pay for them?" Whit asked.

"I think it was about . . . ah . . . I paid $25 for the two of them. There really is not much gold in there without the lens."

In a moment, they passed the samples and the lens back to me, and I put them back in the display case. We said our good-byes, and they left the shop. I watched them walking to their car. They were talking a lot with some hand gesturing.

A week went by, and as we were paying our dinner bill at Charlie P's, Sheldon and Whit came in the place wearing casual clothes. We stayed near the counter where the cashier was. Sheldon said to the three of us, accusingly, "We checked the curio shop at Silverton, and they don't have any free-gold samples like you have."

"Well, they must have quit selling them. It has been a few years since I was there," I said. I made sure that the cashier could hear what we were talking about.

Sheldon continued, "Where was the rock shop in Ouray where you got the other ore pieces?"

"On the east side of the main street. I think it was near the center of a block of shops," I said.

After a moment of awkward silence, Whit said, "The Idarado mine is closed."

I was a bit defensive and said, "Well, I visited the mine quite a few years ago."

We finished with the cashier and moved outside. Whit and Sheldon were rather disturbed with the way the conversation was going, but they finally backed off and soon left us. It was Thursday evening, and we planned to leave for home in the morning for family gatherings.

Friday morning we had a quick breakfast and left Charlie P's about seven thirty in the morning. Eddy and Walt drove off in their cars, but I took the truck back to the shop to get some personal things and a bag of laundry. I left Lake City about an hour later, and when I crossed the bridge over Blue Mesa Reservoir and turned left on US-50, I thought I recognized the Chevy that Sheldon and Whit traveled in just approaching the bridge I had just crossed. The car was a kind of a generic dark gray with no frills. I slowed to about 10 mph below the speed limit, and the car lingered at the slower speed and allowed some other cars to pass. My truck was a big one and very red, but in traffic a mile back, I lost track of the less-conspicuous car. I watched for a chance to make sure they were following me, and when the highway made a quick turn to the south, just after passing the dam on Blue Mesa, it made some quick sharp turns then crossed a narrow bridge at Pine Creek. There was a dirt road that led up Pine Creek, so I quickly turned on the road and stopped just far enough from the highway that I could be seen, but I would not be visible until the following traffic was committed to drive on by. I quickly opened the door and pretended to be relieving myself behind the open door.

The third car to pass was theirs, and Whit was driving. When they had passed my road, Whit looked back, so I was sure they saw my truck. I waited about five minutes, then backed up to the wide area near the bridge and got back on the highway. I did not see them again until I had passed through Montrose and headed north on US-50/550. They must have been parked near the approach to Montrose so that they could see which route I took out of town. When I was certain they were behind me, I called Walt on my cell phone. There was a good signal, and he answered on the second ring.

Walt was pulling into McDonald's in Delta, about twenty miles ahead of me. We considered what to do next. I told him I would lead them to the Amtrak station in Grand Junction and stop at a curio shop there where I knew the owner. We tried to contact Eddy, but phone service is rather spotty in the San Juans. We would have to wait until Eddy got close to Durango before we could tell him what was going on. Walt wished me luck and soon left McDonald's. He still had another 150 miles to get home.

When I entered Grand Junction, I stayed a little slow in the traffic so that Whit wouldn't lose me, and I made a deliberate exit to pull into the parking at the train station. Grand Junction has an elaborate old train depot, but most of it has been abandoned for decades. One waiting room has all the old decor, but only an abbreviated ticket office serves Amtrak trains that come and go a couple of times a day. I stopped near a side entrance to the ticket office. While I was lifting a box out of the truck, I saw the nondescript dark Chevy four-door stop about a half a block away and across the street—but still in view of my big red truck. I took the box into the ticket office. Luckily, the entrance door at the curio shop was open, because the manager only opens a little before and after the scheduled Amtrak arrivals. He calls his place Gemums and Rockums, and he has a small but interesting array of rock samples plus snacks and magazines. He would have very few patrons at that location except for the Amtrak patrons. He does well for only being open a few hours a day.

I left the box inside and came out for another one, then took it inside also. After ten minutes, I brought the boxes back to the truck and drove home. The Chevy followed to my street, but turned away without getting closer than a long city block.

The next Monday, Eddy's family obligations preempted his working that week; but Walt met me after noon, and we drove to Lake City, arriving in time for a late dinner at Charlie P's. A couple of the staff came to the table while we were eating. They were nearly always in the place when we had dinner, and we had visited with them often.

"Who are those two guys that have been hounding you here lately?" the older one asked. He had a dish towel and had been clearing tables when we came in. A name on his shirt said "Nick."

Walt told them that they were asking about our place at the old Joe Banner mine. Nick sat down, and the woman stood behind him. He began a lengthy conversation about the two men. "Apparently, they have talked to the guys at the gas station and the post office and even some of our employees. Maybe others around town." Nick finally asked what we were doing at the old mine and if we were actually selling any ore.

"We're not selling any ore, but we sure are enjoying our time in this area," Walt said.

Nick asked, "Are you actually mining anything?"

"Not really," Walt said. "But Dell here"—nodding my way—"did some probing when we first got here. With today's markets and the smelting business as it is, he was not very optimistic."

"I told those guys almost the same thing," Nick went on. "But what about gold? Do you get any gold?"

"No," I said, "we aren't really getting anything. But if there was gold, we would need a big smelter to recover it."

Our conversation went on a bit longer, but discussion about the mine was limited to the new name we had on the mine entrance. We had to explain that Los Tres Cabras are the three old (retired) goats. Our mine is mostly a retirement center. And Walt is an avid elk hunter, and Colorado has more elk than Utah has. With this property, he can get a resident permit now.

Next morning when we arrived at the mine, there was—stopped in front of the gate—a topless, beat-up, and drab Jeep that might have been surplus from WWII. The skinny kid from the gas station was in the passenger seat, and an older man, possibly his father, was the driver. The two men on the back bench were Sheldon and Whit. I pulled the truck up beside them where I could squeeze by to get through the gate. When the others exited the jeep, Sheldon sauntered behind my red truck; and trying not to be obvious, he casually nudged one of the two boxes I had left uncovered. It was obviously empty. He glanced up to Whit, who had observed his move.

Walt climbed out of the truck and greeted them as he unlocked the gate. I pulled the big red Ram in, and when he started to pull the gate closed, the men in the jeep hustled over to go in with us. Walt was going to lock the gate, but he stopped before he put the padlocks on and said, "We'll let you guys close the gate when you leave." We did not invite them to bring in the jeep. It was only a couple hundred feet to the massive mine door.

Whit went to one of the broken jackleg drills and stood over it with his hands in his pockets. He pushed on it with his shoe, but it was pretty heavy and hardly moved. He glanced at the other one and glanced around at some of the junk I had brought over from the trash at Geneva Steel. He put his foot on the drill again and called over to us. "What is this thing?"

Walt looked to me to answer him. "It's a hard-rock drill," I said.

Whit glared at me a little and said, "Can you operate it?"

"I don't think so," I said. "Not in my condition—they don't call them 'widow makers' for nothing. They are pretty simple machines. But they need a compressor, and we don't have one."

Whit stared at the drill with a puzzled look and scratched behind his right ear and down on his neck. Again he cast his eyes around the junk on each side of the big door, and he kicked an old boot, which had much of the leather worn off the steel toe. We made no move to open the door. His mind was not putting things together very well.

Sheldon was next to try to make sense. "You say you are not shipping any ore, yet you took some boxes home last week," he said.

"What are you talking about?" I said.

"I saw you take some boxes Friday morning in your truck when you left Lake City."

"Oh, you mean those two old fruit boxes that are still in the back of the truck," I answered, sounding a little annoyed at the grilling we were getting. "They're just empty boxes," I added.

Our conversation was not very friendly anymore, and the jeep driver was scuffing the soil nervously with one shoe while both hands were stuffed in his pockets. Walt drew out a ring of keys and started toward the mine door. He hollered over his shoulder. "Please secure the locks on the gate when you leave," he said. "We need to get to work."

"Okay," grunted Sheldon.

The four of them slowly walked back to the jeep while Walt and I entered the mine door and pulled it shut with a heavy clank. After a couple of minutes, I put on a hard hat and opened the big door. I went out to the truck and pulled it into the mine opening. As I tugged on the big door to close it, I could see the guys in the jeep. They had locked the gate, but they stared at me wearing a hard hat and closing the heavy door.

A couple of days later, Sheldon and Whit again met us at dinnertime in Charlie P's.

After casual greetings, Sheldon came right out and bluntly asked, "Come on now, you two. Just what are you up to with your 'mine'?"

"What do you mean by that?" Walt asked.

Sheldon piped up, "We've been asking around, and the guy in the museum says that on 'Hinsdale County Earth Day' a while back, they cleaned all the junk from a bunch of local mines. And your Joe Banner mine—or whatever you call it—was one of 'em. He said he was sure because he was on that particular cleanup crew." After a pause, he said emphatically, "You guys are mining gold up there!"

He had raised his voice enough that patrons at nearby tables couldn't help but hear. Things in the room quieted down considerably.

Walt began to chuckle and said, "We are not mining gold."

"Then why all the activity at that mine?" Sheldon asked.

"It's a cheap summer recreation site," Walt replied, still chuckling. "It's also a great hunting camp until the snow drives us out."

It was obvious that the humor Walt was enjoying was not appreciated by Sheldon and his partner.

"Then why do you have your so-called 'shop' over on Pine Street?" Whit said.

"We can't get to the mine for half the year because of the snow," I explained. "There's not much room in that little place. And the view at the mine is much better."

"And another thing," Whit said. "That other guy with you used to drive an old clunker, and he showed up last fall in a new Mercedes. And you"—he points a stiff finger at Walt—"you've got a fancy new Cadillac!" Facing me, he adds, "And that whompin' red truck of yours . . . You guys are mining gold!"

Their tempers were rising, and Sheldon leaned closer to me and asked sternly, "What are all those trips to Grand Junction with a truck full of boxes?"

"I *live* in Grand Junction! I have a family there. I go *home* to Grand Junction!" I said with irritation.

"But you take the boxes to the railroad depot!" Sheldon said. He leaned back smugly, as if he had just won the argument.

"I don't go to the railroad station," I said sharply.

"You did last week," he countered.

"Who in the world told you that?" I said.

"Because we followed you, and you drove straight to the train depot!"

"You guys are nuts," I said. "That's an Amtrak station, not a freight-train stop."

Going for his final point, Sheldon said, "And I suppose those two boxes you took in the station were just empty boxes, and not boxes of gold ore."

"You really did follow me. You guys really are nuts," I said.

"Why did you bring the boxes back out of the station?" Sheldon continued.

"Because the guy in the rock shop there didn't want any more wood boxes," I said with finality.

"What rock shop?" Whit asked.

"The Rockum and Gemum shop," I said. "He sells snacks and curios, including rocks, to the Amtrak passengers. You should have followed me a little longer."

By now, several patrons and the help at Charlie P's were watching our table in fascination. We were probably the most exciting thing in Lake City for a long time. The story of cannibal Alfred Packer eating five snowbound prospectors near there in the 1800s was bigger, of course; but we had their attention for the moment. Sheldon and Whit did some serious whispering among themselves.

Sheldon looked at us and asked, "Just what would you say if someone offered to buy your nonproducing little gold mine?"

Walt said quickly, "It's not a gold mine, and it is not for sale! Forget it!"

"Suppose we offered you a cool fifty grand—what would you say to that?" said Sheldon.

"Don't be ridiculous," said Walt. "Anyway, it's probably worth more than that."

Sheldon continued, looking very serious through his wire-rimmed glasses, "Let's say you have a mine, and we want to buy it. What price would you ask?"

Walt answered, "It's not a mine, and it is not for sale."

Just then, as if on some mysterious cue, Eddy pulled up outside in his little white Mercedes. He scuffed his feet a couple of times on the floor mat and walked in. Everybody in the place turned, and those that knew Eddy was our partner became even more interested in the scene before them.

"Well, Eddy," Walt said and stood up. "What are you doing here?"

"Aw, Kathy went off to Phoenix to see some relatives, and I thought I would come over." He glanced at the anxious spectators and said, "What's going on? Am I interrupting something?"

I got up quickly and dragged a chair over for Eddy to join us at the table. I said, "These two think we have a gold mine, and they may have offered to buy it."

Eddy laughed. "I hope you didn't sell it," he said as he sat down.

"We're still trying to convince them it is not really a gold mine," Walt told him.

"And we are *not* convinced," said Whit, who had been quiet for some time. "You guys are pulling a fast one on us, and we are calling your bluff."

Eddy looked questioningly at Walt and me. "They are not really serious, are they?" he said.

"You bet we're serious," Sheldon said. "And the offer is half a million dollars."

Walt glanced around at the interested spectators and said, "I guess they really are serious."

I cut in quickly. "Don't be foolish. There is no gold, and we are not selling the place."

"Make it a million dollars!" said Whit.

"I can't believe what's going on here," Eddy said. "What have I missed?"

Walt stood up. Everyone turned to him with no idea whatsoever what was going to happen. He cleared his throat and said, "This is sheer foolishness. We all need to leave and sleep on this for a while. Okay?" He picked up the meal ticket from the table and moved toward the cashier.

There was much shuffling of chairs and some pretty excited chatter until the commotion gradually died down. In half an hour, the place was nearly empty of patrons, and we three pals went back to the shop for the night.

"If they push us any more, what do you want to do?" Walt asked. "Frankly, my wife is pretty tired of my being gone so much. She prefers her home and garden and hates the long drive to come here, and she doesn't like the responsibility of tending our three horses."

"It's wearing thin for me too," Eddy said. "I still need to finish the work on the house in Farmington."

"Well," I said, "my family and especially the grandkids have enough on their plates that they don't like to drive most of two days to get here and back. I live the closest, and the novelty has worn off, for sure."

Next morning was a clear, crisp morning in May. There was still snow around in town, but it was wasting away quickly with the warm afternoons. Parking is always a problem in Lake City because in the winter there is always a lot of excess snow, and the plows work only the main traffic routes. In the summer, the place is always jammed with tourists. Lake City is a virtual mecca for outdoor enthusiasts. There will be loads of hikers, mountain climbers, bikers—both with pedals and noisy motorcycles and off-road machines of every description. A lot of cars have Texas plates because many people in the Depression let their property go for taxes, and Texas was emerging as a wealthy state with oil fortunes. Colorado is about the closest real recreational destination for Texans, and they bought up a lot of the state. Fishing and sightseeing is fabulous in the San Juan Mountains.

For some reason, the tourists had hit the parking around Charlie P's, and we had to park more than a block away. When we stepped inside, Sheldon and Whit were seated at the center table, and there were twice as many patrons as we had seen this early in the place. All eyes turned to us as we came gingerly in and took the three empty chairs at the center table. The room was surprisingly quiet, with few of the normal sounds of eating in a busy restaurant during breakfast. It seemed like we were the main attraction for something ominous like a funeral or maybe a hanging.

Sheldon opened the conversation. "Last night we offered to buy your gold mine for fifty grand, and you said it was worth more than that, but it didn't matter because the mine was not for sale. You told us that it was not a mine, and only a recreational getaway. You made light of several signs that you might be, in fact, mining gold up there and you are secretly taking it out, but pretending otherwise. Now tell us. Is it a valuable gold mine?"

Walt looked at Eddy and then me, and then slowly stood up. He surveyed the attentive group assembled in the restaurant and said, "Nothing has changed since last night. Your offer for half a million dollars was certainly generous, but it is still not a gold mine and still not for sale." He checked Eddy and me, and we both nodded affirmatively, so Walt sat down.

A number of whispered comments went around the room, but nobody stirred for a long time. Whit and Sheldon whispered a few short comments, and Whit slid his chair back a few inches and said, "How about two million dollars—does that sound better?"

I said, "Of course it sounds better, but we couldn't accept money like that for that place. The answer has to be no."

Sheldon started to stand again, but Whit touched his arm and sat him back down, and Whit said, "Just think about this a minute. You guys were kids together, and we know that the professor there"—pointing to me—"is over seventy years old. You men don't have a lot of time to enjoy whatever comes from this venture. If we made it three million, that would be one full million apiece to add to your retirements. What would you say to that?"

The three of us had blank stares for a second, but we recovered quickly. Walt spoke very deliberately. "You would be willing to give us three million US dollars for that mine that has no gold and we don't want to sell?"

"Exactly!" said Sheldon.

Walt said simply, "We would be fools to refuse."

The assembled patrons (and certainly some curious locals) then became very noisy.

It was more than a week before a check was verified and we turned over the keys to the double locks on the fence and the huge lock on the mine entrance. In the meantime, we found out that the County attorney had been in the restaurant that fateful morning, and we asked him what charges could be made against us if the mine had no ore. He said that nobody would stand a chance to convict us after that little scene at the Charlie P's.

We loaded the big red Ram with most of our belongings and gave a lot of stuff to one of the local churches. It was early afternoon when we headed out of town with the Cadillac in front, followed by Eddy's white Mercedes and my big red Ram truck. Then, at a wide spot, before we had even reached the highway speed-limit sign, the Hinsdale County Sheriff's car was stopped in front of us, with flashing lights, blocking part of the driving lane. He stood on the roadside and motioned for all three of us to pull over in the only wide spot available. He beckoned for Eddy and me to come to where he stood at Walt's car. When we were all there, he said, "I've been watching those two guys for weeks, but I never saw them actually break the law. If there is no gold in your mine, you guys pulled off a pretty good poker hand. Come on back for the elk season, okay?"

TREASURE NUMBER 15

ANTS

I moved from desolate Midland, Texas, to western Colorado in 1972 and quickly tried to do everything that can be done in the Rocky Mountains. As a college professor, I had to work most of the summers, but I kept several weeks open each year for play. I bought a canoe and floated all the easy stretches of several rivers, including the Colorado River. Using the canoe, the family all caught fish out of lakes on the Grand Mesa, which is mostly just over ten thousand feet in elevation. With my son, I tried more than a dozen lakes in a single year. I even toyed with the idea of fishing fifty different Colorado lakes in one summer, but only fishing long enough on each lake to catch one fish. I planned to take photos of each lake and the fish and write up the whole saga and try to publish it and make a little money. However, when I started out on the Grand Mesa, the fishing was so much fun on the first few lakes that I settled down to more relaxed fishing and camping and smelling the roses. It turned out that there were more Colorado Columbines (the state flower) than roses, plus a huge variety of other wildflowers. I hunted deer with a compound bow and hunted elk with a rifle. There were also ducks and geese, quail, pheasants, and cottontails that needed harvesting. There were mountains to climb and lots of rocks for a geology teacher to study. I was in heaven.

Some of the rivers are too rough for a canoe, so I ran my share of white water with rubber rafts. One time we scheduled a bonus diversion for our geology field camp, and we took the gang in several rafts down the Colorado River from Loma (only fifteen miles from the campus) through Westwater Canyon, which is a few miles into Utah. We camped one night along the way and had a great time. At the head of Westwater Canyon, we passed the "Old Miner's Cabin" and heard about a guy that mined placer gold there back in the 1930s during the Great Depression. We didn't take time to stop at the old cabin, but I made a mental note to check into the story a little deeper. After passing the cabin, the river gets pretty nasty for a while, and we soon got very busy trying to stay on the rafts and get in the best position to miss the worst trouble spots in the white water. One place is called the "Room of Doom" where the river heads straight into a narrow point (or sliver) of rock, and the flow splits into two channels. The channel to the left is the main stream, but the channel to the right dives into a turbulent whirlpool and the water comes back around and tries to rejoin the main stream. However, the main stream forces it back into the whirlpool, making it very difficult to escape the "Room of Doom." Experienced rafters make certain they are left of center when they approach the place.

Utah's Westwater Canyon Section of the Colorado River

Seventeen miles of popular white-water rafting about thirty-five miles from Grand Junction, Colorado.

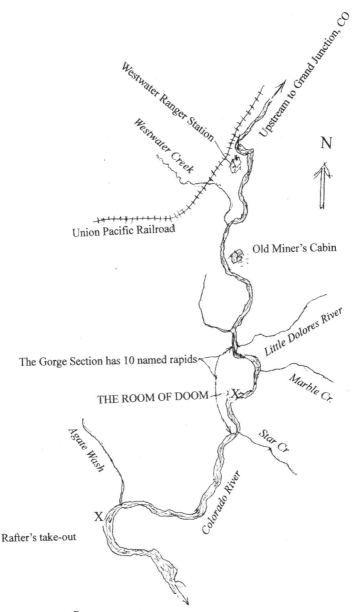

Several years passed, and I learned to pan gold and did a few consulting jobs on some gold placers in Colorado, Arizona, and Utah. When the family went on vacations, I ended up taking some pans along and checking streams in Wyoming, Montana, Nevada, Idaho, and California. I checked streams where I knew there were old gold camps, and most of the time I could get a few colors from each site. My total gold accumulation became a few grams of gold, but I never spent enough time in the good places to get any real "treasure." Most of my efforts were for fun. I even dropped my gold "poke" a couple of times and broke several small glass vials while teaching classes on panning or showing friends how it is done. The gold would only fill the bottom of the vial, but we always kept the vial full of water so that the water would serve as a microscope, and it made the small grains look much more impressive. Once, I dropped a vial which had nearly a gram of gold, probably a month's effort, and it spilled out in some coarse gravel. It was enough gold to justify scooping up a big panload of gravel and recovering it all. A simple task if you knew exactly where the vial spilled. Very few grains were visible in the gravel because the water carried it out of sight among the pebbles.

In the late 1970s, there was a surge in the price of gold, and panning became an obsession with a lot of people. Soon after, you could see people along many of Colorado's streams, trying to recover a few grains. Clear Creek, which runs off the Front Range and comes out in the town of Golden, near Denver, was especially popular. US Highway 6 follows the creek upstream, close to the old gold camps of Black Hawk, Central City, and Idaho Springs. Clear Creek exits the mountains at Golden, Colorado—home of Colorado School of Mines (CSM). CSM is a premier school for mining engineers. On a weekend, there might be several dozen people working the creek. It is certain that students from Colorado School of Mines would know a lot about the area, and some of them might even be among the people panning the stream. Much of the activity was "recreational panning," but a few people were trying to find enough gold to make it worthwhile to stake a claim and try to get some real money from gold.

To get on with this story, in 1979 an engineer from Montrose, Colorado, offered a night class in Montrose on gold panning. About seventy people enrolled. The class was so successful that he offered it the next year in Grand Junction where he hoped to get even more students.

I was a geology professor at Mesa State College, and he was offering a night class in my school. Of course, I attended the class. An astonishing 120 students signed up. There were kids, grizzled old geezers, women, regular daytime students, couples, and families. The man's name was Adamson, and he did a good job. Near the end of the class, he asked me if there was a site on either the Gunnison River or the Colorado River that had some good potential to have the class do the Saturday "practicum" to test their ability to recover placer gold. The Gunnison and Colorado Rivers flow together in the town of Grand Junction—hence the name, the grand junction of two important rivers. I told him that I didn't think there was a good gold-bearing site near town, so he arranged to take the class back up the Uncompahgre River, which is tributary to the Gunnison River. The site was handy to Montrose, where he had done the Saturday practice the year before.

As soon as I told him there was no good site near Grand Junction, to quote the pamphlet I published later: "I knew I was in trouble. I didn't know for sure! I would have to find out." In 1982, I published a fifty-two-page booklet titled "Where is the gold on the Colorado River? And how do you get it out?"

The booklet describes 217 sites between Granby, at the headwaters, and the Grand Canyon in Arizona where I sampled the gravels and panned out any colors I could recover. Only nineteen panloads yielded no gold. The others went from one speck to over four hundred. Most of the specks were barely visible, and required bright sunlight to recover them all. I used a wide-mouth one-liter container (about a quart), and the samples were uniformly about five pounds dry weight. The best one was at a working placer mine at Dewey Bridge, Utah, about fifty river miles from Colorado and a few miles upriver from Moab, Utah. The second best site was at the "Old Miner's Cabin" in Westwater Canyon.

I pondered the results of my little booklet. I had paid about $3 a copy to publish the thing and only charged $3.25 per copy. I didn't make any money off the booklet, but I enjoyed the excitement of the venture. Five thousand of the booklets went quickly, so I did a second printing. That also went quickly, but slower than the first printing, so I let it go out of print sometime in the mid-1990s. I got involved in a more ambitious publication of a textbook for my class on the geology of Colorado. I had not become rich writing a booklet about gold panning.

The Old Miner's Cabin site is a tough challenge. To get to it to sample it, I went downstream by canoe from the road that ended in the small community of Westwater. In the 1980s, there were a few farms and an "office" for the US Bureau of Land Management (I think that was the agency). Topographic maps showed some primitive roads in the area, but access was very questionable because of private ownership and the possible designation of that stretch of the river as "wild and scenic"—which would limit the activity that can be conducted at the cabin. For sure, it had some historic value. After my sampling venture, I had to paddle and drag my canoe back up to the end of the road in Westwater because I knew I could never run the rest of Westwater Canyon in a canoe. That run can be challenging for expert rafters, and some lives have been lost in this section.

My panning trip to the Old Miner's Cabin was with a couple of Boy Scouts, and we had a sort of picnic lunch while we were there. I was glad for the scouts because it gave me a little more "power" to get the canoe back to the roads. While we sat with our lunch in what little shade we could find, I noticed some of the wildlife. We saw some chipmunks, rabbits, prairie dogs, noisy magpies, ravens, and some songbirds. Geese and ducks also used the river. A couple of hawks were catching a thermal a short distance downstream. However, there were a lot of loud flying yellow-winged grasshoppers and a variety of insects, including gnats and abundant mosquitoes. After our lunch and some pleasant minutes of enjoying the natural surroundings, we cleaned up our gear and prepared to pole the canoe upstream to the pickup truck. We had spilled some of our lunch stuff on the upside-down cardboard carton we had used for a picnic table. There were some ants—some little brown ones smaller than a grain of rice, which had gathered on a smudge of peanut butter and strawberry jelly from one of the boys' sandwiches. I called the little brown ants "sugar ants" because they looked like the same kind that somehow keeps getting into our kitchen in Grand Junction. Some big-jawed red ants, common in the western deserts, were working on a small piece of chocolate-chip cookie; and two huge black ants that I see often in pine and alpine areas were trying to drag a piece of rind from a slice of summer sausage that was to go in our trash to haul back to town. I call the big black ones "timber ants" because I only remember seeing them where there are needle-bearing trees. It seemed odd that the three species of ants had no apparent interest in the booty that each of the other species had selected.

Driving home, the boys dozed off to sleep in the crowded cab of my mini-truck. When I got back to I-70, for the last forty miles or so, I thought about ants. I really THOUGHT about ANTS. How can ants find stuff to eat so quickly? When we started lunch, we saw no ants. In a half an hour, we had foraging crews of three different kinds of ants busily gathering their special food supplies. The big ants could have taken all the sweet stuff from the little ones. The biggest ones probably could have taken the cookies from the red ones. Maybe the big jaws of the red ants kept the others at bay from the cookies. Maybe the big black "timber ants" were more carnivorous and were after the meat sticking to the sausage rind. Their jaws were pretty impressive too. Forty miles on a lonely, hot freeway in the desert allows a lot of ant thoughts.

Ants crossed my mind often in the following months until I saw a TV special about ants on some science channel. The TV show included a segment about a species of ants somewhere in the world that raises a fungus that they harvest to feed the colony. The colony selects certain larvae to become foragers that go out and harvest flower petals. Another group of larvae are prepared as mulchers. Their job is to chew up the petals to make a pile of "stuff" that becomes the select habitat for a fungus, which is then harvested for the colony to eat. A portion of the colony is specially bred from select larvae to be larger and have powerful mandibles to become protectors of the whole colony. The same queen lays all the larvae, but somehow ants can prepare harvesters and mulchers and soldiers from the eggs of the same queen. From the start, each new ant knows exactly what its job will be in the colony, and they rush to do their job as soon as they can move effectively. Ants are amazing!

I had experience with termites when I was in high school and worked with a local pest control firm in Ogden, Utah. I knew that termites could "make" workers and soldiers. I remember lying on my stomach in the crawlspace under a termite-infested house and watching the colony protect the workers by sending big-jawed soldiers to protect the little white workers as they tried to repair the damage I was doing. The termites build sandy tubes on the cement footers that support the walls of the house. This gives the workers protective cover to get at the wood in the house.

The little soft white worker termites will not move in the open air, so they would soon bring a mouth full of "saliva cement" to patch the tube when I would break a section of the tube. Immediately after I broke the tube, the workers moving up or down the tube would check the opening and back away from the open air. Shortly (and as I remember it, in less than a minute), the hard brown jaws of the soldiers would poke out into the open hole. Quickly, some little workers would start stuffing some new cement into the breach. I remember putting the corner of a piece of paper near the breach, and a soldier would immediately snap his mandibles firmly onto the paper. I could remove the soldier by withdrawing the paper. I could collect a large number of soldiers by this method, and I collected a couple of jars of sample termites to take to the pest control office. My job at the time was to break down all the tubes that gave the termites access to the wood in the house. I would pump a solution of sodium arsenide in a powerful jet onto the surface of the soil under the house, making certain there was plenty of arsenic solution all around the footers. I recall one of the homes that had been sprayed years before but had become infested with termites anew. We found a patch of the soil under the house that did not get enough of the arsenic solution, and the termites had made a sort of castle more than three feet high that connected the soil with the bottom of the flooring in the house. The termites had made a freeway to the wood.

The TV show about ants prompted me to buy an ant colony. I wanted a bunch of those big red ones, but my first attempts could not find any of that variety. My friend in the biology department at the college said they were generally known as Western Harvester ants, but somehow that didn't sound right compared with some really unique ants in some jungle that I have seen featured in science videos. They were called "harvester ants." My friend also suggested that I could find what I wanted at Ward's Scientific or Carolina Biological Supply House. I soon was overwhelmed by all the stuff you can do with ants. I wasn't planning to get another degree or two in some aspect of entomology. I just wanted to work with an ant colony. I finally found a cheap price on a genus *Mystrium* from a tiny island between Madagascar and Mozambique. After I got to working with them, I became a little nervous about the fact that the genus lives in a tropical environment at only about fifteen degrees south of the equator, and I was planning to work with them in a drier climate at nearly forty degrees north of the equator. Maybe hindsight is a little clearer than my barging into something I am not qualified to work at. When I started, I just figured that ants are ants. Enough said!

However, the more I got into my plans, the more unqualified I felt.

Mystrium ants are an ugly lot. These sketches are about
eight times natural size. The one with the large mandible
is a soldier ant. The other one is a worker.

Anyway, I found that I didn't have an "ant farm" because that name is copyrighted. If you study the ants in a colony, you are a myrmecologist, and you are working with a "farmicarium." My ants of the genus *Mystrium* are really ugly ants—but the price was right, and I was having more fun playing with the colony than I was trying to become a legitimate myrmecologist. I tried testing them with a variety of foods. I tried half a dozen kinds of bread crumbs and a variety of fruits. I even used some cocoanut and mango, but the ants generally ignored my offerings. I was hoping to find a food that I might use to train them to bring me a special kind of sand grain, and then I would reward them with a choice morsel of something they liked to eat. You might be able to see my twisted logic in trying to get a colony of ants to become retrievers of something special that would be in the range of the ants that would be foraging from the colony. I thought if I could sprinkle some fine gold dust in the area of the colony and then watch carefully if one of the ants brought me a gold speck and I could reward him, I had no doubt that the ant would figure out a way to tell the other workers in the colony that the gold grains would bring them choice food. I wasn't having any success in finding a choice food to lure them to work for me. I was also losing some ants in the colony. I only saw a few dead ones, but they would only remain a few minutes. I couldn't tell whether the colony ate the dead ones or not because I think they were taking them back "underground," but I could not ever determine where in the tunnels the dead ones went.

After many weeks of toiling with the colony, one of the grandkids came to watch me at my "work," and he spilled a couple of crumbs of gingersnap on my table. I tried a small bit in the colony, and a couple of the little workers grabbed hold of the cookie and dragged it into the colony. I became quite excited because I thought I had made a great breakthrough in my grain-training with the ants.

My next step was to partially block a tunnel with several small grains of gold. Gold weighs nearly ten times as much as a sand grain of the same size, so I couldn't use very big pieces for a single ant to move. When I put the gold in the tunnel, I prepared a bit of gingersnap to drop near the gold if the ant moved the gold out in the open to get it away from the colony. In less than a minute, I had a dozen ants mining the gold out of the tunnel, but I couldn't get them to notice the gingersnap that I dropped near the place where they deposited the gold. And they each deposited the grains in vastly different places. The little guys moved so fast that I was usually confused as to which ant I should try to reward in time for it to get the message.

I worked for at least a week trying to teach the ants that a piece of gold would deliver a bit of gingersnap, but I never could make it work. I had used so much time to get this far that I was beginning to lose hope that I could ever train an ant colony to work for me.

When you buy an ant colony, the supplier sends some food for the ants, and they will eat it. In the beginning, I tried some of the food; but much of the time, the ants wouldn't get the food when I provided it to them as a training device. I even tried starving them by withholding the food, but it only made them slow down their work, and I found some weak and dead specimens when I tried the starvation plan. I stopped quickly when I realized that the queen needs more food than any of the others, and I wouldn't have a colony if the queen starved to death.

All the time I played with the ants, I kept checking stuff on the Internet to learn more about ants. One day I saw an article that said some ants would haul away dead ants from the colony and put them in a separate refuse pile. After much study about "how does an ant know another ant is dead," the conclusion was that ants release a pheromone when they are alive, and they stop releasing the pheromone when they die. So a dead ant "smells" differently to his colony. Instead of "stinking" when he dies, he sort of "unstinks" quickly after dying. What if I could scent up a bit of gold with the stuff that remains when the ant dies? Maybe I could get the ants to remove the gold from the colony and pile it in a remote refuse pile. When the ant brought the scented gold to the refuse pile, then I could reward him with a bit of gingersnap.

I assumed that most ants use formic acid in their bites to cause the painful burning sensation that I have felt often. Because I was only guessing (and didn't have the sense to ask my biologist friend), I smeared different parts of ants on many gold grains over a long period of time. I didn't think formic acid would be involved in the pheromone, so I used separate parts of ants to get away from the acid. Parts of the head did not give any positive reaction, and the abdomen didn't work either. It seemed to me like the middle (thorax part) was only a series of articulation joints, but I tried it any way. Eureka! When I dropped gold grains in the tunnel that had been stirred with a bunch of thorax portions, the ants picked up the gold and put it all in a remote place on the surface as far away from the entrance to the colony and the container would allow. After cutting a large number of my precious ants, I found I could stir whole dead ants with the gold, and the ants would still haul the gold to the remote site. Now I was making progress. The gingersnap was unnecessary!

But if I have to use gold that I have already found to make the ants bring it back to me, I hadn't accomplished a thing. I wanted *them* to find the gold in the first place. After some frustrating weeks, I began to stir the dead ants for a shorter time, and I used fewer dead ants. Finally, I had the ants returning gold to the remote corner of the colony's box that had not been touched by recently deceased ants. I repeated the operation many times, and the ants began to quickly move gold from the colony to the remote site. I used several samples of gold dust to make sure the grains I had trained them with were not the only gold they would collect for me. It worked consistently! I think I was ready to go "mining" gold at the Old Miner's Cabin at Westwater Canyon on the Colorado River just inside the Utah border with Colorado.

I bought a used three-man rubber raft and stopped shaving in February so that I could look like an old geezer looking for gold. When the time came, I loaded my ants and plenty of food and enough camping gear for a long stay on the river. I figured April tenth was a safe time to start the operation so that my tropical ants would not get chilled if a nasty cold front came through. I got some extra tarps and my old catalytic heater to make sure I could keep my ants warm. I even took three boxes of gingersnaps, for just in case.

Communications at Westwater posed a problem. There is a cell-phone microwave tower near the little town of Cisco, Utah; but down in Westwater Canyon, I was not sure that I could get phone reception. I arranged with Jim Johnson and my nephew Walt to contact some of their old river rats that still run rafting tours through the canyon. Jim was our department chairman and was eventually made dean of the School of Natural Sciences and Math at Mesa State College. He was still the short and lively fireball that I first met in 1972. Now his hair was as frosty as mine, but I think he would have liked to go camping on the river again. My nephew Walt was living in the Denver area, but I knew he still had friends in the rafting business because he had to leave a day early when my wife died and the family was all together at Grand Junction. His emergency was a long-awaited river trip that he was helping with, but I can't remember which river it was. Jim and Walt gave me the names of Pete Swenson and Eric Blogstedt, who promised to at least stop at my camp each time they went down the river. There would be more than a week sometimes between visits—but my family could send word if there was a need, and I could report to the outside world if an emergency developed.

April 10 finally arrived, and my son Paul had some serious misgivings as he pushed me into the river at the Westwater BLM boat ramp. He drove me to the site so that he could take my pickup home. It wouldn't be safe at such a remote place for weeks at a time. His opinion was that I wouldn't be safe there for weeks at a time either. I told him that all the stuff that usually breaks on older guys had already been replaced or fixed, so he was not to worry. I even patted my .22 revolver that was holstered on my side. "For the bears," I told him. I was sure that I could frighten a bear away by shooting the gun—not that I could stop one if

I was attacked. I told him that my biggest concern would be the small rodents that would try to steal my food and the insects that would pester me constantly. If I had to leave my camp early in the season, I would be pretty anxious running the fast water alone during spring runoff, but my intentions were to leave in September or early October when my precious little *Mystrium* ants had collected a few pounds of gold dust. I packed six one-pint screw-cap plastic bottles for my intended gold poke. A pint is 16 ounces, and if gold is nineteen times the density of water, a pint of gold dust might weigh 19 lbs. Dust is not a solid mass, so I must account for some pore space in the dust; so let's go for 12 lbs. per bottle. Twelve pounds each in six bottles would be 72 lbs. of gold. At over $900 an ounce, my summer's effort might net me over $60,000. Before I had time to plan where to spend my sixty grand, I was at the Old Miner's Cabin and beached my raft and set about organizing my camp.

My setup would have to look like I was panning the river gravels for the summer, so my ant colony would have to be secure from the summer rafters that might want to make a short stop at the cabin. I didn't expect many visitors because the rafters are after the thrills of white water and keeping out of the famous Room of Doom. My camp is only a short ride from the boat ramp at Westwater, so most of the rafting bunch would not want to stop so soon. It was possible that only messengers, Pete and Eric, would ever stop. What I didn't want was some fool Western-history buff looking for some neat historical place to write about. One of those might spoil my adventure. I also hoped the BLM officers were not too eager to exercise undue authority over me. I was sure one of them would run the canyon occasionally. The adventurous part of the canyon is only a few miles, but to drive from the BLM station at Westwater to the pick-up site below Cisco is a lot of wasted road miles for the BLM office to pay just to check on the short canyon.

In less than two days, I had my tent up, a nice fire pit, a large pile of firewood, a couple of extra stone stools by the fire for my company, and a new home for the ants. The ant colony was in a box the size of a small suitcase, but I wanted room for the colony to expand. I didn't want to lose the queen if the colony went deeper, so I brought enough light wood to build an ant-tight box three feet deep and 3×4 feet at the top. I sealed all the wood joints with duct tape in case the box developed some leakage during the work season. I buried the box to the brim and, using my panning screens, I filled the big box with sand from the river sediments, hoping to get a few grains of gold in the box. Then I removed the bottom of my ant colony and placed the colony gently into the larger box of sand. If the colony decided to expand their crowded home, there was plenty of room. I even hoped they would enlarge their army of workers for me. The queen would have to decide that.

When the job was finished, I stepped back and admired my work. Soon I would have a hundred or so hardworking ants gathering gold for me. About two feet away from the opening for the colony, I placed a little saucer full of sand with a piece of gingersnap on top, just in case the ants might put my treasure in the saucer and take some of the cookie as reward. The trouble was, there were no ants. The day had been warm for April, but probably colder than the Madagascar tropics. I rigged my tarps and the catalytic heater to heat up the air for a cooler night. The colony had spent the first night under the raft, and I had put some stones that I had heated by my fire under there with them. In the heat of the day, I saw a couple of ants when I moved the box to the big sandbox. I knew they were still in there, but they were not checking the outside now at all.

My second night was worse than the first. It was at least ten years ago I promised myself I would never sleep on the ground again. With iron knees, a fused ankle with screws, and straps in my back and a crib in the spine, I need a stool or post or something to assist me when I try to arise in the morning. Not to mention at least two visits to the outside in the middle of the night. I checked the heater under the tarps, and it was a cozy warm temperature. All seemed OK. I began a breakfast routine that would be an unconscious habit for the coming months. My day would be a few hours of panning gold, some good reading of a stack of books, and a lot of sitting alone in the shade and being grateful for life in a wonderful world full of geology. My wife of nearly fifty-five years had died unexpectedly of leukemia with only four weeks of warning. Life on the river now was lonely, but otherwise a sort of Shangri-La. Now if the ants would just get busy and make me financially secure, I would be in my utopian heaven on earth.

After a week, I could see no gold coming out of the deep sand in my box. The ants were beginning to forage away from the environment I had made for them, but they were not harvesting any gold. I brought a four-inch reading glass so that I could watch my little workers with enough detail to see what they were doing. A lot of vegetable stuff was being taken below to the colony. It looked like bits of leaves, but I was never sure. Some nondescript brown stuff, which looked like coffee grounds, came to the colony every time I watched. Occasionally, there would be parts of dead insects. At first, I never saw my ants kill any other species, but they were bringing in a harvest of critters. One day, four ants in a row marched up to the colony, each with one of the little brown "sugar ants" that I had seen years earlier when I first sampled the sediments at the miner's cabin. I watched others entering the colony from the same direction, and I followed the troop back into some sagebrush where there was a war going on. My *Mystrium* ants were attacking a foraging party of the sugar ants and removing the victims to the colony. Usually, two or more of my ants would attack a single sugar ant, but I saw more than one incident where a single *Mystrium* would defeat a sugar ant. My ants were a little bigger, but obviously more ferocious. Possibly, the brown ants were not the fighters for their colony.

It was my thirteenth day of camp when I noticed a little extra activity on my saucer of sand with a piece of gingersnap. The ants had taken a lot of gingersnap to their colony. I had to add more cookie every couple of days, although it was only a crumb the size of puffed wheat each time. I hoped the colony had some conscience and would soon pay for the cookies with some gold. I studied the activity for a long time, but each new ant that came to the cookie site did not appear to have any gold in its mandibles. I knew the gold would be very fine, but with my reading glass, I figured I would be able to spot a bright shiny piece of gold in the sunlight. I was getting a bit desperate because my "mine" was not working. In my frustration, I took the saucer down to the river and carefully panned out any heavy grains in the saucer. There was some black sand which I knew was mostly magnetite, and it was heavy enough to help me control my panning technique to make sure I was saving all the heavier stuff. Gold is more than three times the density of most of the black sand minerals. In the few seconds it takes to work down a small saucer full of sand, I expected the possibility of a single speck of gold, maybe two. After all, I had documented two hundred specks at this site in my little book on gold panning along the Colorado River that I published back in 1982.

Surprise, surprise! I carefully counted twenty-seven specks, all of them in the "very fine" range—the ones you need bright sun to see with the unaided eye. Because I had caught the sand in a smaller pan as I panned out the sand in the saucer, I had all the original sand. I was not certain my ants had brought any gold to the saucer, because I did not clean the sand before I had put it in the saucer in the beginning. I replaced the saucer with the same sand I had just panned. Now there was definitely no gold in the saucer of sand.

I gave the ants two days to go back to their routines in the colony. On the second day, there was again some activity at the saucer. I removed the saucer and panned the sand again. To my delight, there were eleven tiny specks. I put a bigger crumb of gingersnap in the saucer. My "mine" was working!

After my thirtieth day in the camp, the gold recovered by the ants was equal to the gold I had panned by my own work. It was a paltry two grams. I was guessing at the weight, but I had a carefully measured gram of gold in a vial that I kept for comparisons. The ants had produced about $20 in gold in a month. I too had recovered $20 worth of gold dust. I was getting about 15 cents an hour for tedious, backbreaking effort in the hot sun on a lonely riverbank—and I was overjoyed! My ants were only gathering a fraction of a cent per hour, because they were working more than fifteen-hour days.

Production from the ants began to taper off rapidly, so I guessed that the nearby sediments had been scoured thoroughly. I used my little shovel to stir up the sand for about forty feet around the colony. This would give the ants access to virgin sand at the surface. I was careful not to destroy the vegetation in the area because the BLM would be justified in citing me for disturbing the natural environment with no permit to do so. Scuffing the open sand would hardly call attention to my project. It only took the ants ten days to match the production of the first thirty days. My summer was barely started, and I had "mined" about $50 in gold. The colony seemed to be raising more workers, and the days were getting longer. One trouble was becoming more evident. I had stirred the surface sand so many times that I guessed that I would have to stir it deeper or move the colony to a new site.

While I was checking my surroundings, I looked back at my saucer of sand and saw a horrible development. Some big red Western Harvester ants were attacking my little *Mystrium* workers on the saucer with the cookie crumb. I dug through my camp gear and found a small pair of tweezers. I went to the colony and began to catch the red ants and smashed them on a paper plate. The fight was furious! Mandibles on the big red ants are strong enough to bite my tough fingertips, even on the hard fingerprints.

I was making a big difference in the battle, but more red ants were coming, and they were pretty hard to catch with tweezers. There were a number of my little workers being hauled back to the red ant home. I followed the line of the new red warriors back to an anthill that was at least two hundred feet from my camp. I used a stick to destroy the anthill. There were ants all over the place. I received several bites, but the nest seemed to be focused on rebuilding the mess I had made. I stomped on the trail of red ants that led to my little colony and scraped much of the trail so that later ants would have trouble finding my colony again. For good measure, I built a bonfire on the red ants' hill and kept it burning for several hours. A couple of days later, Pete Swenson brought a party of rafters to my camp, and among other things, I asked him to bring me a turkey baster so that if the red ants came again, I could fight them better. I could suck up the offenders a lot more efficiently with a baster rather than tweezers. The last incident cost my colony a lot of workers. With the red-ant raid resolved, it was time to move the colony.

It was going to take a lot of work. The plan was to do it at night when the foragers were all in the colony. First, I had to dig a hole big enough to hold the large box. I filled about half of the box with sand because I expected the colony would be a lot bigger than when I first planted it back in April. In the evening when the workers were home, I carefully removed the original ant colony. I had trouble keeping it intact because the colony had expanded, and I broke the network of tunnels which had been added at the bottom. There was no sign of the queen or her nest. She must be somewhere in the new construction that was in the bottom of the larger box. With only a single lantern to light my task, I was able to remove all but about a hundred pounds of sand. It was obvious that I wrecked a lot of tunnels, but I must have missed the queen. I hoped I had not crushed her. I had a lot of angry ants trying to fight my operation, but with a lot of grunting and struggling, I slid my box up a gentle ramp and moved it to the new hole. When I was finished, I was afraid I had ruined the whole project. I didn't dare cover much of my mess, lest I smother my colony. I gave up about four a.m. to get a little sleep. In the morning, I added a little sand to make a ramp on one end so that the ants could get out of the big box. I could add a little sand each day to finish filling the box, but not enough to smother my little workers. When the sun was up enough to warm the place, there was a lot of activity in the box. There was a lot of repair work to be done.

In five or six days, the colony was approximately back to normal. Nothing happened for several days at the saucer of clean sand and a lump of gingersnap. Nearly a week passed before I saw any ants at the new location going to the saucer. Eventually, there were a few. They came from the surrounding area in twos or threes and separated by as much as an hour with no ants at all. After four days of what seemed to me very light activity compared with my original system, I took the saucer and panned out the contents. There were only twenty grains of gold. Most were small, but there were several that were considerably larger. They were still very tiny grains, but noticeably larger than at the former location. That was good news and bad news. There was more gold to be harvested there, but I was very worried about my ability to move the colony again.

By mid-June, my project was humming as well as it did in the first location. My ants were more productive than before. The gold was a little coarser, and they were finding a few more grains each day. My ants were producing twice as much as I could in the three or four hours I devoted to panning each day. My back could not handle more than an hour or so at a time. I had nothing better to do each day, so I kept at the panning. Even with the ants, my daily take was not a reasonable salary. Living was cheap. My reports from home were that my utilities were at record low cost because my yard was not getting much water and I was not tending my usual garden. Pete and Eric kept my bills coming to me, and they even brought me some checks to sign, and my son was good to send me all the important stuff for the summer. Most of my transactions at the bank were done by direct deposit, and I was surprised how simple life can be when you don't have to drive around all day and play golf and go out to dinner. My diet was pretty drab at my camp, and I was probably losing weight. I could use a little of that. My original supply of food only lasted about a month, and I was getting resupplied one box at a time using the "Pete and Eric Express"! I missed my friends and my church too, but it was like a temporary assignment in the military when I was out of contact with my usual family and friends. I'll admit my routine at the camp was boring. Pete and Eric started bringing me special treats. Sometimes it was some cold milk or a sack of apricots.

The rafters all had ice chests, and Paul sent me a six-pack of Mountain Dew one time via Eric. Wow, what a delight.

By late July, my ants were having trouble finding gold in the nearby sand, and I had stirred the surface a dozen or more times. Each day, I hauled sand in my two buckets from various sites around my camp. I was getting weary of all the work, and production was slowly declining. To get a bucket of sand required some strenuous shaking of my screens to get rid of about 80 percent of the old river gravels. The sand (and gold) was only the matrix of the river sediments. If you try to pan sediments that only contain sand, usually there is no gold because a stream current that only transports sand is not strong enough to dislodge and move much gold. With production declining and my disappointment with all aspects of the project, I was considering calling it quits. I would not have a single pint of gold dust. My $60,000 treasure would be closer to $600.

When Eric came through on July 23, he said, "Four of my party didn't show, and I think you need a break. Why don't you ride on through with me and I'll bring you back with my next load, which will be Friday?"

That was only three days away, and I agreed to go with him. Eric checked my life jacket to make sure it was an approved model. It was dusty and badly used, but it passed his inspection. I told him it had been on at least a hundred fishing trips in my canoe. In less than twenty minutes, his four passengers helped me aboard and we were on our way.

Skull Rapids was a little tense, but once we were through that, the Room of Doom was a "piece of cake" with Eric on the oars. In fact, the river was so low that the Room of Doom was not even a hazard. It looked like a peaceful little eddy where you might relax and make a few lazy circles while you pop a cold one and maybe eat a sandwich. He positioned the raft in the tongue of smooth water just above the rough stuff and, twisting a little to the left, he made it look as easy as parking your car in your own driveway. The wedge of rock that splits the current went by smoothly on our right side, and it did not seem as dangerous as I had remembered. When I last went through, I was a young and impressionable young man, and it was during spring runoff. Late July was not so challenging.

My business at home needed only one of the three days I had, and I must admit it was nice to be back in civilization. My first shower in four months took more than forty minutes. By the time Eric was ready to return to the river, I was getting very impatient to see my little ant friends. We drove all the way to Westwater to put into the river. Eric chose to meet the other raft in his party at Westwater. They went in at Loma, Colorado, and spent the night at Black Rocks. We took two passengers from the other raft and drifted quietly down to my camp. Before noon, I was alone again at the Old Miner's Cabin. I went downstream the few hundred yards to my ant colony and found it empty. The ants were all gone. I checked as well as I could to see if predators had destroyed them, or if they left on their own. There were no dead ants and no apparent damage to the colony. I carefully dug down the couple of feet to where the queen should have been. There was a large empty den. There were no eggs, no larvae, and no evidence of any ants. I was saddened to lose my ants. My emotions were mixed a little because there was some relief that the project was over and I could go on with my life. I was slowly beginning to forget the $59,000 that I didn't make on this venture. I decided to wait until the next morning to leave my camp. There was no point getting to the pickup site below Cisco at night because it would probably be vacant.

Saturday morning was quiet and somber. I dug up the wood box and burned it. While the box and a couple of other waste items burned, I broke camp and prepared to go home. I kept the original ant colony box and carefully packed my raft for the short run to the take-out beach. I doused my fire with a bucket of water and pushed out into the current. I could see that my left oarlock was loose, and I decided that I would be wise to pull into the bank and retie two ropes to snug things up. The right bank of the river had a better place to beach my raft, so I pulled in there. After fixing the oarlock, I walked up on the bank to relieve myself. I looked back upstream where I had spent the last few months. It was still a beautiful place for a geologist. Watching my feet to avoid stumbling on a rock, I noticed a small anthill. I instantly recognized *Mystrium*. They are ugly!

Now what do I do? I watched the few ants I could see to figure out what they were doing. They were digging a new colony. Only a few at a time came to the surface, each with a grain of sand—or in some cases, a larger chunk of rock. It is always amazing how much an ant can carry. I guessed that my colony of ants had nursed a new queen. The old one might have died, or perhaps the colony started working on a new batch of queens and had destroyed her. How many other queens had been nurtured? Were there other colonies on this side of the river? I wished I knew more about ants. I knew that termites produce a batch of winged adults, and there is a mass emergence from the colony, and the new flying termites (or "winged adults") spread out to find new quarters. When a suitable place is found, they shed their wings and go about the same old process of producing a variety of termites to manage a new colony. I wandered more than an hour on the north side of the river looking for new anthills. There were several western harvester hills, but no more new ones for *Mystrium*.

Apparently, this new nest of *Mystrium* had just arrived because there was very little material on top of the ground. What did the old colony teach the new ants? Could they mine gold? I sat down on my raft and munched a granola bar and took a long drink from my water bottle. Should I try my experiment again? Or should I go home and have a nice dinner with my kids and grandkids? I could last a week easily with my remaining supplies, and Pete and Eric would be able to supply me just as they had before. I was so curious about those ants, I made my decision. I dragged the raft up on the bank and started all over again.

This time, it would be easier. I didn't have to worry about cold nights; nor did I have to bury a big wooden box to keep the queen from going too deep. She was on her own this time. After pitching my tent and making a good fire pit, I dragged in a good supply of firewood. When my camp was established, I dug out the saucer for the gold deliveries and found my cookies. I panned a small sample of sand and removed three small specks of gold. I dried the remaining barren sand and placed it on the saucer with a crumb of gingersnap on the top. I would wait a week to see what would happen.

Over the next several days, I panned numerous samples upstream and downstream from my camp. The gravel is not as abundant on this side of the river as where my old camp had been, but there was much less vegetation on this side, so the access was better for my little ants. It would be easy to scrape up a fresh batch of sand for the ants to work with. However, I found it was much harder for me to pan on this side of the river because it is steeper, and it was tough to make a place to sit in the edge of the stream without slipping in. The old miner at the Old Miner's Cabin had great access to the river. The old guy had built a cabin, so he probably made his own access ramp there.

On day six, I decided to check my saucer. If there was no gold in it, there was no point staying another day. In the few seconds it takes to check about a cup of sample, I mused about what I would do if there was some gold. It didn't take long! I quickly exposed a tiny string of gold specks. They were still very small. You need sunlight to see them with the naked eye, but there had been no flecks when I put the sand back in the saucer. The little guys were trained! If anything, they were better at the collecting than the first colony was. Mandatory school in an anthill is better than anything I have seen in my life. In a few days, we have a small army of perfectly trained workers. Marine boot camp can't even do that.

By now, I was no longer dreaming of $60K, but I would like to fill part of a bottle with gold. When Pete and Eric came, I gave each of them a list of items I would need to last another month. They were perfectly willing to do it. I settled down for a month or so of patient supervision of my little ants.

I had a number of things that I would have to resolve back at home before about September 10. All the stuff I had been postponing since April would become critical by then, so I planned to leave after the first week of September. Nights would start getting cooler by then, and the very productive early work on the surface of the sediment would be slowing down by then. I had no plan to dig up the colony. It would be almost impossible to dig deep enough to get the queen safely removed and get her colony through the white water and back home to Grand Junction. She and her colony would have to perish. Certainly six months of winter—including snow and a lot of ice along the riverbank—would kill a colony of tropical ants. Whatever training the new ants were getting would not prepare them for the coming seasons.

August went by quickly and with unexpected production. Instead of the ounce of gold I got before the colony left the first site, I had more than half a pint of dust before September 1. I checked the bottle often, and just to heft the thing was very satisfying to me. I guessed it would be worth $4,000 or more. I had personally panned less than $100 worth, and it had been a lot of tedious, tough work. My ants had made a very interesting venture a somewhat prosperous one too. A long summer job that pays only $4,000 is pretty sad for a former member of the American Institute of Professional Geologists (No. 3331)—but for a feeble, old retired geezer that spent a pleasant summer on a remote riverbank among some great geology, it was rewarding enough. I still wished it would be $60,000.

August had been rather idle for me. Panning on the steep bank was tough, and I was pretty burned out with the effort with such limited reward. During the Great Depression, there were a lot of men made a bare subsistence from panning gold at places that were not much better than at the Old Miner's Cabin. Many of them had no choice. It was work for meager rewards or starve! For me, however, I was spoiled with a pretty good retirement. My kids were all grown, and my wife was gone—what was better than making a little money in gold? Well, maybe making a lot of money in gold. At least, I tried.

With only a few days left in August, I got the bright idea that it might be more profitable to take a colony of ants to Arizona, where I know of some spots with more gold, and a lot coarser than on the Colorado River. One of the best places I knew about was a few hours' drive over horrible roads east of a little community called Oasis, Arizona, which is just inside Arizona east of Boulder Dam. At Oasis, you turn out into the desert toward Senator Peak. There is no water there, but the ants don't need much water (if any). My mind started thinking stupid again, like when I first conceived the idea to mine gold with ants. But my ants were already trained. If I could keep the colony alive, there was a chance to recover more gold and a lot easier. Logistics would be a mess, but I could use a pickup instead of a small raft. I could pack in enough water and food to go a couple of weeks at a time, and it would be easy to drive out to Boulder City from time to time. Kingman, Arizona, might be even quicker.

Somehow I convinced myself that it was worth a try. I started planning my exit from the Colorado River venture and prepared to test my system in Arizona. The key was to keep my ants alive. I waited until the fourth of September, and then began to dismantle my camp. The first step was to try to dig the queen out of the new anthill. I dug down about two feet and made a trench about two feet away from the opening of the anthill. With a little digging, I encountered a lot of ants on all sides of the opening. They had spread much wider than I guessed. With a zillion of my precious ants scrambling all over the trench and my tools and even me, I broke into an open pocket in the trench on the upstream part of the circle. I was lucky I saw a bit of a cavity before I jammed my shovel into the queen's chamber. I was getting some bites, and I was having trouble extracting any of the surrounding material around the chamber. With a lot of frustrated digging with a short shovel and a rock pick, I brought out about a cubic foot of somewhat consolidated sandy soil from the trench and put the whole mess in the original box for the ant colony. I never could see into the chamber, but when I finished the extraction, I checked all the nearby soil and did not find anything better. I hoped I had my queen. With the base and top on the box and enough sand to make the box about like it had been when I bought the thing, I gathered a lot of the scurrying ants and put them in the box with the others. That step was not easy because every time I tried to slide the top open a little, the ants tried to escape. Also, the ones I was trying to add to the box didn't want to go into the box. When I had a good army, probably enough to prepare a good new home, I closed the lid and packed things for the trip home.

My "poke" of gold worried me. A number of people had seen me on the river for the whole summer. They could see I was panning gold, and they probably figured I had quite a bit or I would have quit and gone home. I still had my pistol and my skin was pretty dark, and I had an awful mess of hair. I had not shaved or trimmed anything, and I looked like some sort of a wild, crazy man. I suppose I was pretty crazy, although I tried not to act too wild.

When I got my "stuff" out from under the raft, I flipped it over and was pleased that it had not lost much air. I puffed on it until I couldn't push any more air into it and punched it a couple of times to test the firmness. It was as good as on my first day on the river. I still worried about my poke. When I was loading all my gear, I looked at the five empty plastic pints that I had brought for the rest of my $60,000 "poke." If I filled the extra five bottles with sand, maybe I could hide the one with gold in the bottom of the box with my leftover food items. It was the only security I could think of. With the rafting season winding down, my worst problem might be to get back to Grand Junction after I pulled out of the river below Cisco.

I checked my cell phone, which had only been turned on a few minutes when I went home for that weekend in July. I had recharged it then, and it appeared to be fully charged as I was getting ready to cast off. There would be a possibility to call Grand Junction from somewhere near Cisco, and I could get my son to bring my pickup and haul me and my gear and the raft home. I had already told Pete and Eric to warn my son Paul that I was coming out in early September.

In the process of breaking camp, I noticed that the water in the river turned a little murky, as if a storm had put in some more mud upstream somewhere. That is typical on the Colorado River because most of the tributaries are in arid terrain, and a summer storm can change water that is clear enough for fly fishing into chocolate milk. I think "Colorado" means "color red" in Spanish. Much of the time, the water is pretty colorful. I pulled the raft a little higher on the bank as the water came up a foot or so. It is possible some additional water was being released from Blue Mesa Reservoir on the Gunnison River, which is the main tributary for the upper Colorado.

I was ready to shove off a little after noon, and no other rafters had come down that day. I would have to go alone through the rest of the canyon. The water was still rising, but was still much lower than the scary spring runoff that fairly roared down the canyon on my first trip. When Eric brought me out in late July, the flow was pretty peaceful. I expected even less trouble in September, but right now the river must have forgotten that it was supposed to be more peaceful in September. When the flow is low, the boulders are more numerous. The water is not so swift, but the boulders on the bottom are no longer covered with several feet of soft water. It looked like I might have a near medium flow.

As I got closer to the Room of Doom, I started looking for the rocks that Eric told me to watch for so that I could get on the left side of the channel. Nothing looked the same in the deeper water, but the key ledges and boulders were very distinct, and I spotted them easily. Skull Rapids was a bit tricky, but I managed to ease through them like an expert. The extra gurgling of white water adds to the excitement in this part of the river. I was doing fine. Things were getting a little testy, but I was in full control and pleased with my progress so far. As I approached the Room of Doom, I could see that today it was not a peaceful eddy to pop a cool one and eat a sandwich. It looked pretty spooky, and the smooth tongue was not very smooth.

I pulled hard on the right oar to align the raft to face the right place to clear that sharp wedge in the middle. I didn't want to go into that swirling mess on the right side. Suddenly, my right oar jammed into a rock and lifted me off my seat before the oar snapped. I was close to the right place, but I couldn't straighten the raft in order to go down facing forward. I flailed the water with the good oar, but I went sideways into the wedge of rock that splits the current. When I hit the wedge, there was a sickening scrunching sound, and the raft started scraping up the wedge of rock.

In a terrifying few seconds, my little raft was standing on top of the current, impaled on that wedge of rock and shuddering horribly. All my stuff poured out into the torrent. I lost the left oar and scrambled around on the side of the raft, trying to shove myself off the raft and into the left channel. The shuddering of the raft got worse, and I heard more scraping that sounded like a loud version of the bare thighs of a swimmer sliding into or out of an inner tube. The flow was sliding the raft toward the right channel. I pushed off the raft with all the effort I could muster, and the raft flipped upside down and went spinning into the Room of Doom. I was underwater and smashing into rocks with my shoulder and legs and got some hits on my head. My life jacket was not helping me much, and I was terrified that I was not going to come up—maybe never! All I could see was murky brownish water, and I was not sure which way was up. The few bubbles I could see were swirling in all directions: up, down, and both ways around. It may have been less than twenty seconds, but I was almost gone when it became lighter in one area, and I pulled for all I was worth to get to the top.

My life jacket pulled me up quickly when I got clear of the turbulent water, and I spluttered to the top, gulping all the air I could get. I was out and in the clear. I could see none of my stuff. I assumed the raft was still turning around and around upside down in the Room of Doom. I finally saw the broken blade of a paddle drifting in the fastest part of the current and probably more than a hundred feet downstream. I decided I was OK. My right hip hurt a lot, and I had a bad lump in the middle of my forehead. The outside bone on the right ankle hurt, and both knuckles were roughed up badly. When I held them up in the light, the back of both hands were bleeding. Fortunately, my injuries were painful but not very serious. It didn't take much effort to stay in the deep water and away from rocks, so I just drifted along for quite some time. The water was surprisingly warm, and I was not chilled at all. During spring runoff, the water is too cold for swimming, although a lot of the rafters insist on trying. They don't stay in the water long.

Below the fast water, the river runs through a series of beautiful canyons with vertical red, orange, and pink walls of sandstone. As the canyon widens, the current slows. I began to get a little anxious about getting through to the pick-up beach. I was probably drifting as fast as a raft, but it seemed like forever. It would have been a rather pleasant experience if I had not gone through such terror to get into the river. I was very tired.

After floating for several hours, I could smell smoke and eventually heard some voices. Finally, I spotted people near a couple of big pickups with trailers for hauling rafts. They obviously were waiting for some rafters coming along behind me. When a youngster near the water spotted me, he started shouting to his party near the trucks, and quickly I had a gang of people at the water's edge to help me. One grizzled young man with a plaid shirt and a battered floppy felt hat asked me, "How many of you are there?"

"I was alone," I squeaked. My voice was almost gone. When I reached knee-deep water and tried to walk, I could barely stand up. Many hands quickly steadied me, and as soon as I hit some dry sand, I had them let go and I flopped to the ground. The warm sand felt good, and I realized I was shivering. The guy with the floppy hat stayed with me, and I became aware that he was one of the rafters with the pickup trailers.

"What happened?" he asked.

"I broke an oar above the Room of Doom and hit the wedge sideways. I think my raft is still in the room, upside down."

While we were talking, someone waded out and picked up an oar in the shallow water. He came toward me and asked, "Is this one of yours?"

"Yes," I said, "and part of the broken one went down ahead of me." No one had seen it. It is probably against the bank someplace.

Before I was ready to try my legs and stand up, a group of three rafts came in with about six people on each one. They had seen my raft in the Room of Doom, and they were afraid some of the occupants were still in the water up there. One of the oarsmen came over to me and said, "Are you the guy that has been at the Old Miner's Cabin?"

"Yes."

The guy with the floppy hat came over with a GI ammunition box with a big red cross on it. As he opened it, he turned my face up and looked carefully into my eyes. "You don't look too good, but I don't think you have a concussion." He held the box toward me so that I could look at the mirror taped to the lid. "Is that you in there?"

At first, I wasn't sure. The guy in the mirror had a big lump above the bridge of his nose and was purple clear to the outside of both eyes. Both of my shoes were gone along with one sock. My "nurse" with the floppy hat put some disinfectant on my knuckles and on the scuff on my right ankle. He dabbed something into a small cut in my scalp that was trying to ooze some pale red water, then he wrapped my hands and told me that I was "good to go."

"Do you need a ride?" he queried.

"I think so. I don't think my cell phone will work." I was fumbling with my wet pocket where I could feel the phone.

"There is good reception here—but only with a dry phone." He noticed mine was dripping wet.

Someone loaned me a phone, and I arranged to meet Paul at the first Cisco exit off I-70. I was told that after a while, a crew would try to recover my raft with some special gear designed just for that purpose. There was no promise when that would happen or what the chance was that they could recover it, and I didn't care. I don't want to do any more rafting.

Treasure Number 16

THE CUTE SENORITA FROM COLOMBIA

After my wife died, I continued to go to dinner with three other couples who had been close friends for years. One in the group had a close friend who was a delightful waitress at the local Dos Hombres restaurant, and they had a special where you could get your second meal for half price on Mondays. We tried other venues, but some of the gang preferred Dos Hombres; so there we would meet at five p.m. every Monday. Occasionally, one or more couples couldn't make it, but we also had a few party crashers among our mutual friends—so dinner at five became a ritual over the years. It was the social highlight of the week for some of us.

Probably my best friend in the group was a former corporate pilot for Total Oil Company in Michigan; his name was Dick. He had been a sailor on a destroyer in WWII and was strafed by a German fighter somewhere near Italy. I would have expected him to hate planes and pilots after that, but he became a very active civilian pilot without military flight training. He was an instructor in the old Stearman biplane and in T-6 trainers for many years and did charter flying in Michigan before the job with Total Oil. Some of his work was with Lear jets as well as several twin-engine commercial planes that were represented with classic models adorning his den. His wife had died when he was about fifty. His pal died about the same time, leaving his lovely widow, Sandi, alone. As they had been associates for years, in time, Dick married the widow Sandi. They fit nicely among my friends in Grand Junction, and Dick and I spent a lot of our idle time sharing stories about flying. I flew multi-engine planes and served a tour in Korea in the 1950s plus a few years with artillery spotter planes in the National Guard. I even built a homemade plane that I finally had to sell because of my low salary as a college teacher with five kids. Dick and Sandi were close to me and my Sherry, and we did other things together besides the Monday dinners at Dos Hombres.

My Sherry developed leukemia and, with little warning, died. Dick and Sandi were a great help for the tough weeks after my wife died, but only five months later, Dick died from some lingering medical problems. Before Dick passed on, he had some weeks where he was too weak to join the Monday dinners, and Sandi came alone—so the two of us were almost a couple at the dinners. When Dick was gone, we really were a "couple" at Monday dinners. We even added a few Thursdays with just the two of us alone. Things went pretty well, but Sandi was charming and several years younger than I, and eventually she began coming to the dinners with an RV salesman that seemed to have a lot more zip than I had. He was younger.

Monday dinners continued, and the relationship with Sandi and the RV salesman matured to an engagement, and I could tell that at the dinners I was becoming sort of an "odd man out." And one week when I was going to go on a cruise, alone, to the Panama Canal, I jokingly announced: "I'll show you. I will go find me a cute little senorita in Acapulco." I was about to drop out of the dinner group anyway.

My "cruise" started with a short hop to Denver, then another to catch the ship at Los Angeles. While waiting to board the flight out of Denver, another passenger sat near me that I had seen a few rows ahead of me on the first flight out of Grand Junction. In our short conversation, she said she was catching a cruise ship at LA. She was a pleasant enough woman, but sadly, she was meeting an old girlfriend for a cruise bound for Alaska.

My good luck returned when we were seated in 14A and 14C on the plane to LA. Nobody came to sit in seat 14B. In the hour and twenty minutes between Denver and LA, I discovered that she was a charming widow and a nurse in the community hospital in Grand Junction. Her name was Ada, and after some discussion of my dinner group, she agreed to be my "cute little senorita from South America" at the Monday after my two-week cruise. She doesn't speak Spanish, but she knows some nurses that often go to Cartagena to do charity work there; so that could be our joke on my dinner group at Dos Hombres.

When I got home from my cruise, we had a couple of days to work on our little ruse. She helped me a lot to cook up a real yarn. Let's say that Ada had a rich friend who is a Colombian contractor. The story would be that one day he was working in the emerald mines for the guy that manages the Museo de Esmeralda in Cartagena. There was a serious accident at his mine, and the contractor was badly injured. After a few fruitless weeks of rehabilitating his crushed body, the hospital gave up on him and sent him to a clinic to die. Ada was at the clinic and dedicated most of her time trying to save the injured man. Everyone in the mining camps knew the contractor as "JJ." His name was Jacinto Gonzales Jacinto, and he had two other proper names in there someplace, but he went by Jacinto Jacinto. It should be "Ha-SEEN-to Ha-SEEN-to," but he enjoyed being simply "JJ."

JJ survived solely because Ada tended him. She broke his fever with all-night vigils using cool wet towels. She didn't spare the scarce medicines for him, and there were countless hours of back massage and repetitive motion in his legs and arms to help him recover some mobility. Much of Ada's work on JJ was pretty vague to JJ because he was so near death for so long. The rest of the staff at the clinic told him most of the story of what took place for the first two years of his recovery.

Ada eventually returned to the States before her husband died in 1997. She heard occasionally from JJ, and the reports were very good. He was released from the clinic; and although he couldn't work, he managed to care for himself in a small—and almost cool—upstairs apartment shaded by one of the few trees near the old Spanish dungeon in Cartagena. The dungeon now serves as the bright yellow *mercado* (more like a flea market) for the huge tourist trade that keeps Cartagena bustling.

I should have been suspicious about Ada. I should have noticed how attentive she was when she learned that I was a geologist with some experience with gold. I told her about this book of gold stories, and somehow she nudged the discussion to gemstones. I told her of my experiences at Topaz Mountain and how I would find the little crystals by facing toward the sun and watching the ground for the glint as the sun hit the crystal faces when the sun was at just the right angle. I mentioned that near Topaz Mountain, when you drive the dirt roads with the sun out, you could see the sparkles from a car moving along at 40 mph. Roads and trails often have feldspar cleavage faces that sparkle, and even quartz crystals when sandstones become metamorphosed with enough heat and fluids to grow crystal overgrowths on the tiny sand grains. Some topaz crystals might be nearly half an inch across and have more perfectly flat crystal faces than the cleavage faces on feldspar. With a hardness of 8 on Mohs scale, the crystals could travel a long way from the source with very little abrasion. Softer feldspar and quartz get rounded much easier.

I got home from my cruise, and Ada and I caused a little sensation at the Dos Hombres dinner. However, before we all separated, we had to admit that the whole story was a fantasy—and Ada ("My cute little senorita from South America") had actually gone to Alaska with a friend. Sandi was not very impressed, and I think her salesman was a little annoyed by our behavior.

Ada and I sort of forgot that our "date" was just a joke. When we parted at Dos Hombres, the others cordially invited her to come the next week for dinner again. I didn't contact Ada during the week, but when I arrived for dinner, Ada was already there chatting away with Sandi and her salesman. The others came for dinner, and we all had a great time. Ada was almost the center of attention.

Soon, Mondays were routine for us. I even took Ada to a concert. She met my son's family, and she turned out to be a whiz at our version of racehorse pinochle. Sandi had never made it to our pinochle parties. But I was cautious with Ada because I was still a little miffed at Sandi because she moved on with her salesman so quickly after I thought we were an issue. We could be good friends, but nothing serious for the time being.

One day at about nine a.m., Ada called me on my cell phone while I was at my local City Market grocery store. She excitedly asked me where I was because my car was not in my driveway. I told her that I was next to the bananas at City Market. She said she would be there in two minutes.

I put down the four bananas that I had selected and looked at the bread shelves for a moment, trying to decide what loaf to get. I glanced toward the cashiers and heard some commotion outside the front door when a customer had the door open. The clerks were watching anxiously. Ada stopped her car, blocking the bike racks, and dashed out of the car without closing the door. She rushed into the store before I could get to the door. When she saw me moving toward her, she ran toward me and fairly shouted, "I need to go to Cartagena!"

"That's wonderful," I said. "Are you going to take the cruise again?"

She gave me a stern look and said, "No, I don't have time. I'll have to fly."

"When are you going?" I said.

She answered quickly, "If I can get to Miami by two p.m. tomorrow, that is when I will go—otherwise, I have to wait for Saturday."

I could see that she was troubled—and very nervous about what was going on. "Why such a big hurry?" I asked.

She stared down for several seconds at the white knuckles of her clenched hands and, biting her lip, she slowly looked into my eyes with big tears starting to flow in her own.

"Do you remember the injured contractor named JJ—in Colombia?"

"You mean the guy in that crazy story we cooked up for the dinner group?"

"Most of it was not just a crazy story—JJ is dying!"

I laughed slightly and said, "You're kidding."

"No, I am not kidding. The museum director just called me this morning."

"Hmmm," I stammered a little. I was very surprised. "Are you going to try to help him again?"

"No, it's too late," she said. "He is too old and frail."

Stumbling for words, I hesitated a bit and asked, "Then what possible good can you do for him?"

"I just have to see him," she said. "Even Saturday might be too late."

My practical nature kicked in and I said, rather sternly: "That is a lot of risk, trying to get hurry-up tickets to go that far when there is a good chance you won't make it in time. I'll bet it will cost over a thousand bucks to get there on such short notice—and that's only one-way."

She snapped back, showing some real anger. "The money doesn't matter. I just have to see JJ before he dies."

"Okay, okay, you have to see JJ before he dies. You'd better get started making some phone calls. It seems to me you are being irrational."

She sniffed her nose and wiped her eyes with a hanky. "Dell, you have to come with me!" She blurted it out, and a gush of tears flooded her eyes again. She dabbed them some more with the hanky and mopped her cheeks. Her eyes were red and glistening.

"But, Ada, I can't just drop everything and run off to South America—that's crazy!"

Anxiously, she said softly, "I can't go there alone—not to Colombia. And you are the only man I can turn to."

"No, Ada! That's ridiculous!" I said.

"You have to come," she said. "You are the only man I can trust."

"What does this have to do with trust?" I asked. Then I added, "I don't have thousands of dollars to waste on a stupid run to South America that will be too late anyway."

She let the tears spill to the floor and said, "It is *not* stupid—and I will pay your way. Please, you must come with me."

"You don't have that kind of money either," I said. "Forget it."

She grabbed my upper arms with both hands, and her nails dug painfully into my flesh, and she blurted out, "If we get there in time, I just might have enough money."

A couple of the store employees were heading toward us, and I took her hand and we hurried out of the store to some shade on the side of the building. They followed us to the door but did not come outside. They knew we were talking about something serious, but they must have sensed that there was a lot of emotion but no anger.

"Come on, Ada—what in the world are you talking about?"

"It's JJ," she said.

"Well, what about JJ?" I asked.

She quieted some and mopped her eyes again. Slowly and very deliberately, she sniffled and said, "JJ's nurse, whom I know, was with the museum's manager. And she told me that JJ has something for me, but I must hurry. JJ said it is VERY important, and she said the VERY twice!"

"Did your nurse friend tell you what it was?" I asked.

"No," she said, "JJ wouldn't tell her, but we have to hurry because we need to get to Miami today. I am going to make some calls now, and if there is space, the best connection leaves Grand Junction at twelve forty-eight today."

I was totally stunned. She was punching numbers on her cell phone that she already knew, and she was asking for two tickets. I had a church responsibility and was doing a birthday party in two days for a grandson, and I . . . I . . . What was I trying to convince myself for? I am not very important at my age and station. I cared enough for Ada that I didn't want her dumped alone at the airport in Cartagena, Colombia. Even two of us would face some risk if we had to move around much—especially if it were dark.

"Hurry!" Ada practically shouted. "Go get your passport and a change of clothes—we have about twenty minutes to get to the airport before security closes."

"No way," I thought. It takes twenty minutes to get to the airport without finding my passport and a change of clothes.

I rushed home. I fumbled with my cell phone while I dug out my passport with my left hand. I left a message for my son: "Paul, please pick up my car at the airport. I am going to Cartagena, Colombia, with Ada right now. I don't know when I will get back, and airport parking is atrocious. Can't talk now. I'll try to call you from Denver or Miami—thanks oodles!"

When I slammed my car door shut at airport parking, I heard another door at the end of the parking line and saw Ada running ahead of me toward the door to the terminal. I thought she was in her sixties, but she looked like a college track star in some kind of suitcase shuttle event. We got our cases cleared, and I headed upstairs to security. They turned me away because I hadn't presented my photo ID at the counter and—duh—no boarding pass. Scrambling down the stairs (happy that it was not an escalator), I passed Ada on the other stairway. From the ticket counter, I turned again to the stairs to go back to security. I was gasping, and the pulse in my temples was frightening. Without a handrail, I probably would not have been able to climb to the top stair.

I hobbled on to security and frantically waved my hand to have them hold the line open, and by the time they confiscated my small pocketknife and I got my metal knees and ankle pins cleared and my shoes back on, the security people were all gone and they were calling the final boarding call for the plane. Ada was standing at the gate, and they had held the plane for us. At Grand Junction, we had to walk out on the tarmac to get to a little turboprop, and I was so weak on the stairs to enter the plane that the flight attendant came halfway down the stairs to give me a hand.

Ada waited at the plane's door and said as I entered, "I think we made it!"

I called my son from both Denver and Miami. He was furious that I was doing such a foolish thing with no warning and no planning. I kept telling him that I didn't know why Ada had to go to Cartagena, but it must be important. We had a little more than an hour at Denver, and I needed most of it to go from one end of the terminal, where the little shuttle goes, to the other end where the bigger jets are.

We idled away most of a day in the Miami terminal, and Ada became more anxious by the hour. She tried to call her friend in Cartagena several times, but with no success. She was guessing that there was confusion there because JJ might already have died.

We landed in a steady drizzle in the dark at Cartagena. There were occasional lightning flashes both eastward (I think) and westward, but they were at a considerable distance. We stepped out of the terminal into the steamy tropical air. The temperature was about 80 degrees, and the humidity was even more with the rain. I was grateful for the rain because it cools things a little; but the humidity is always worse with rain. A line of taxis was waiting, in spite of the predawn hour, and Ada quickly gave a driver the directions to her charity clinic.

JJ was dying all right, but he was still alive—although just barely. Ada managed to stir him awake, and it was a full minute before he was alert enough to recognize her. Blinking and with a little groan, his eyes cleared and he tried to raise his hands to hold Ada. She took his hands and laid them back to his side, and she bent down and gave him a kiss on the cheek. She kissed his cheek again and again, and his groan became a distinctly grateful whimper. His eyes were streaming tears, and he was obviously very happy to see her. Ada dabbed at her tears with a tissue from a nightstand as they mumbled to each other and spoke softly, using a lot of facial expressions and eye movement. It truly was a touching scene. I stood by quietly.

When I could see some light in the sky outside, several people began moving about the clinic, and some fresh white uniforms began scurrying about for a shift change at the clinic. JJ directed Ada to the small table near the bed. The single small drawer had a meager few items in it. If it was the whole of JJ's life, he was now very close to nothing. I guessed that his small apartment would be similarly empty. Perhaps some clothes, but maybe not. The old familiar phrase of "dust thou art, to dust thou returnest" sure applied to JJ. He was approaching the inevitable dust.

He whispered, "The green one." There were two small spiral-bound notebooks. The brown one was old and full of Spanish writing, but the green one was newer and with most of the pages torn out. Of the few remaining pages, only one had any writing. It read "Pablo" on one line and "Museo de Esmeralda" on the second. The bottom right corner had a simple "J.J."

After some emotional and teary cheek-kissing and hand clasping, Ada left JJ and we walked out into the steamy morning of Cartagena. The "Museo" would not open for another hour, so we walked a while in the streets. There were no cruise ships in the harbor, and the street vendors were pretty scarce. Neither of us trusted the food on the streets, and it was a short walk between the clinic and the Museo, so we went back to the clinic to get some food. Ada knew one of the staff who got some juice and some pastries for us. We were stalling for the museum to open more than to get much food.

At opening time, we peered into the museum. A woman saw us at the door and quickly glanced to a clock across the room and got up briskly to come to unlock the door. She wore an elegant satin blouse that was such a dark maroon that it was almost black. She was thin and pretty, with short black hair and simple silver earrings in a small whorl pattern with a small emerald in the center of the whorl. There was a silver ring on each middle finger to match the earrings, including the emeralds. The ring on the right hand had a small cluster of four stones. For an emerald museum employee, she was lovely but certainly not flamboyant. Ada asked for Pablo. The attendant went to a back partition and called for Pablo.

Pablo was short, pudgy, and very crisp, with flashing black eyes and some well-trimmed curly black hair that was giving way to some white on the temples which had invaded about half of the rest of his head. He wore a bright green short-sleeved satin shirt under an open white lab coat. We could read "Pablo" on the shirt; and to me, it resembled a shirt for a bowling team. I was sure it was not for bowling. I guessed he made jewelry, and there was a lot of that on display in the museum. Some was for sale.

Ada showed Pablo the little green notebook.

"Hello, Ada. Did you find JJ okay?" he asked.

"Just this morning," she said.

Pablo asked, "Could he talk?"

"Barely," she answered.

Apparently Pablo had met Ada when she was nursing JJ after his accident. She told me later that she was not sure she remembered him.

As Pablo asked us about our flight to Cartagena, he led us back to a well-designed "mine" mock-up in the rear of the museum. We walked through the short dank tunnels, past the various lighted peepholes that showed raw emerald crystals in the rock matrix of the ersatz mine. On the left wall near the end of the tour was an unlighted "mine adit," which was the entrance to a narrow door that was painted black with phony rock pasted to it. Inside a small room, Pablo turned on a bare light that was hanging on a cord from the ceiling. The light was quite bright for the small room. Some cases of Pepsi cans and probably beer cans lined one wall, and there were some crackers and snack foods on top of a small refrigerator at the end of the room. To the right were two very old wooden dynamite cases. Those sturdy old boxes were familiar to me as the stenciled labels were clear: "Hercules Powder." I hoped they did not contain any old, unstable nitro dynamite.

Pablo lifted the top box and placed it on a bench near the light. On the lid, boldly written (perhaps with a felt marker) was "J.J." Pablo raised the lid, and we could see that the box was only about half full. There were some photos. A pretty girl was in some of the photos, plus a smaller boy that leaned on crutches and might be mentally handicapped. A very pretty woman and the two children were in one photo, which had a nice metal frame.

Pablo said, indicating the photos, "JJ's family. They're all gone."

There was a cigar box full of letters and postcards, some of them with postmarks as old as 1944. There was a coffee cup from San Francisco and a number of black-and-white photos of mining scenes, probably in Colombia. JJ's young smiling face was in some of them. Near the bottom of the box was a small leather pouch with a drawstring on the top. Ada opened it to find a dozen or so of old US tax tokens. Some were colorful plastic ones, and some were little aluminum 1 percent tax tokens that were common in the war years of the 1940s. I was startled to find two Spanish doubloons. Two genuine gold coins dated 1796. I was fascinated and showed them to Ada and Pablo.

Pablo nodded and said simply, "Yes, I know."

I scratched my head and figured that those must be worth a few hundred—maybe thousands—of dollars today. In the bottom of the box was a Panamanian flag and an old and battered flag from Spain. Under the flags was a thin layer of cardboard which I started to remove, but I noticed that it was quite heavy. I turned it over, and it was a sheet of cut emeralds stuck to the cardboard. They were all smaller than half an inch, but there were twenty-seven of them.

I showed them to Pablo. Again, he said, "I know."

Ada was stunned as she raised the card to the light.

We laid the things back into the powder box, and Pablo carefully exchanged the box we had examined with the other box, which was obviously much heavier than the box with the photos and other memorabilia. He fussed a little with a handmade hasp and finally raised the lid, which apparently was a hinged, improvised addition to the powder box. It squeaked as he opened it.

The top had more photos, this time mostly color prints of JJ and scenes of people and equipment in the mining business. A couple showed JJ with a short guy wearing a suit. I looked closer, near the light, and saw that the short one was Pablo. I showed the two shots to Pablo. He smiled again with the standard: "Yes, I know."

A bit more junk, and I got down to another cardboard sheet. I was almost afraid to turn it over. It turned out to be just a blank piece of stiff cardboard. I have often thought that really valuable stuff has a sort of karma, and I used to blame such a power for the excitement I got looking at gold. Actually, I am infected with old-fashioned gold fever. Just now, it seems to be emerald fever. I was getting pretty excited. Just to see stuff like this, even though it was not mine—we were looking at genuine treasure. Well, at least the other box had treasure in it.

Under the blank cardboard was a folded burlap sack, and under it and filling the bottom half of the old Hercules box was raw emerald material—the stuff that the recovery crew picks out of the washed concentrates that passes along a dripping conveyor screen. The light at the conveyor would be very bright, and the good stuff is "high-graded" and put into a secure pile. The recovery crew would be a few trusted workers. The room would be encased in a lot of steel, and there would be armed guards from this stage until the emeralds went on to be graded, faceted, and sold.

Some of it was just amorphous green junk. A few were nice crystals, and some stunning ones approached the size of my thumb. Most were poor quality with fractures, but all were genuine emerald material. I picked out a few larger pieces and held them close to the light. I guessed there was thirty pounds of emeralds, and at least 20 percent of it was what I—now an expert with two minutes of training—would call "good stuff." Valuable emerald material here would be measured in pounds, not carats. Oops! Pardon me. It would be in kilos; after all, we were not in Gringo land.

When Ada's excitement had calmed down and we were finished looking at a fabulous pile of green stones under a bright light, Pablo put the lid down, closed the hasp, and dusted off his hands on his lab coat. He looked at Ada. After several anxious seconds, he said, "Well, what do you want to do with it?" He gestured that he was talking about both boxes.

Ada stammered a little. "Wh-what do you mean?"

Pablo said simply, "JJ wanted you to have it."

Ada's voice was trembling. "But it is yours—and the museum's."

"No." Pablo spoke much more sternly this time, "This is eighty-two years of JJ, and he wants you to have it."

"What can I do with it?" Ada said.

Pablo smiled. "That is up to you. I am so relieved that you were able to see JJ."

Ada was speechless. She looked blankly at the boxes and back to Pablo, then to me. Her mouth was open, and she was absolutely incredulous.

For half an hour, Ada argued with Pablo about the boxes, but his voice and words never changed. It was clear that JJ wanted Ada to have the boxes. Finally, we asked Pablo for a safe place to eat nearby, and he assured us that in daytime, you can safely go any place in town. We meant if there was a safe place without stomach bugs in the water, food, and ice.

"Oh yes, for the Gringos—the bugs of the belly." We all laughed a little, but Pablo could tell we were genuinely concerned about good sanitation in Cartagena. He led us to the front window and pointed the direction for a couple of choices of quality places where the food would be okay for our foreign tummies.

After a couple of hours and a good feed from an undecipherable menu, we had some fish and chips with a side of *camarones* (shrimp), and we were ready to move on. We walked back to the clinic, hoping JJ could give Ada some counsel about disposing of emeralds in Colombia. Ada always talked about "our emeralds"—not "the emeralds" or "her emeralds."

Back at the clinic, JJ was not in his room, but we found him in a sort of ICU room with a couple of nurses and several other critical patients. The staff let Ada see him because her nurse friend vouched for her work as a nurse at this facility some years before. My PhD doctorate doesn't cut me any slack in the medical world, so I was ushered out. Ada didn't return for half an hour, and then she was tearful and shaking her head to the side. I knew it was bad news.

"His feet are getting blotchy," she said. "And he is out of it. He wouldn't make a sound, and his breathing is much more labored. I'll never see him again." She fought the tears.

We sat on a bench near the entrance to the clinic until Ada could walk without stumbling, and then we walked slowly to the museum. We had decided to leave the boxes with Pablo on consignment—and whatever he could do with the gems, he could send Ada her share and take for himself a handsome percentage for disposing them for her. We trusted him because if he wanted to cheat her, he never would have contacted her in the first place. I was concerned about getting the boxes through customs and security at the airport, and even more concerned about finding honest people to work with the emeralds in the U.S. The huge price for bringing so much value into the U.S. was more than I wanted to face.

Pablo had placed the two boxes inside the front door for us, ready for us to take them on our way. We explained our decision to leave the stones with Pablo, and he began to laugh.

"There is no duty on raw gem material. Just take it home."

Ada and I are much better friends now. I still consider the emeralds to be hers, although the Hercules boxes are in my basement with cards nailed on them that say "Ore samples for Mesa State College." Nobody knows the truth about them. We have sold some "stuff" to an artisan in Bozeman, Montana, and to another in Santa Fe, New Mexico. Those two want much more material, but so far, we see no need to hurry. Twenty-six pounds remain of the thirty pounds and four ounces we started with. Ada loves her new car, and she has retired from nursing. The staff at the hospital tried to talk her out of leaving when another two years would give her a much more generous retirement. But she told them she was tired of the rat race, and she would have to cope with a little less for her retirement years. She is buying her new house on a twenty-year mortgage.

The fortune is not mine, and Ada is just a good friend that I happened to meet on a plane to Los Angeles one time.

Treasure Number 17

TUESDAY MORNING HEADLINES

Nostalgically driving westward across the oh-so-familiar Mancos Shale desert of eastern Utah, along the Bookcliffs beyond the dusty town of Greenriver and over the San Rafael Swell, I was on my way to meet a lady I had contacted on the Internet. My wife had passed on two years before from leukemia; and as I drove in silence along I-70, I became unpleasantly aware that in my long lifetime, I had not accomplished much. I wasn't very good at anything. Getting through college required me to work part-time and summers at numerous jobs, including a pest-control service, topping trees, fighting a forest fire, grunt work at a golf course, and night shifts in a hospital as a "psychiatric aide." For a few years, I was a hydrographic engineer for the Utah State Engineer's Office where I did plane table surveys of water diversion points and irrigated acreage.

I did a stint in the US Air Force and some more time as a pilot in the Army National Guard at Salt Lake City. I got married and started a family along the way. I was a good student, but not an excellent one, and graduate school was pretty tough. I ended up with a PhD and went to work for Exxon as a geologist. I guess I was a good geologist, but not remarkable. I didn't fit the industry mold very well and quit the oil business after seven years and got a job teaching geology and weather at a small college in Grand Junction, Colorado. I once was a good pilot, but not a great one. I wasn't good enough to be a fighter pilot—but anyway, I preferred to fly low and slow so that I could look at the geology on the ground below. At least, that is how I rationalized my time as a military pilot. I had made a run at several careers and got along fine. Let's say I was "excellent at being mediocre" at everything I tried. Most of my life, I had looked on the bright side of things and was generally happy and fun-loving.

But on this day—all alone and grinding away the miles on a hot afternoon in July—I was feeling more than a little depressed. My health had been slipping downhill, and I was having trouble with excess weight. My knees and ankles eventually got sore enough so that even walking was painful. That is tough on a geologist. I endured knee replacements, a serious back repair, and a fused ankle. A nasty scar from the navel down several inches testifies of bladder stones and diverticula. Here I was, old and wrinkled, driving a small twelve-year-old car that my deceased wife had inherited from her parents. I should quit kidding myself. I wouldn't be much of a prize for the lady I was going to meet, and I was not sure I cared anymore.

My driving was becoming a bit erratic, and I was getting drowsy enough for a break, and I needed a pit stop. I decided to pull off at the rest stop on I-70 at exit 86, about five miles east of the summit of Salina Canyon. When I pulled off the freeway, I could see that the rest stop was across the freeway and a considerable distance back to the east. When I stopped, I noticed a little road that cut back to the east so I wouldn't have to go over the freeway and all the way back to the rest area. With so little traffic turning off, I could do a quick pit stop and nobody would even notice. I was out of sight from the highway and would have plenty of warning if someone else chose this minute to take the same exit. It would save me several minutes.

I slowly turned down the little road. It was paved at first with what looked like leftover blacktop material from the highway and then gradually deteriorated to two tire lanes with a few little green plants in the middle at first and, finally, substantial weeds between the tire lanes. I stopped and stiffly got out. Positioned behind the car, I sprinkled the rough blacktop surface and surveyed the place. Most of the vegetation was sagebrush, about chest high, and it smelled rather pungent. So many years I have thrashed about in sagebrush. I must be getting old if I am nostalgic about a pungent weed. I have trudged through the stuff looking at rocks as a geologist in probably a dozen states. There were rabbit, deer, pheasant, and even duck hunts that got into sagebrush.

Collecting fossils in Utah, Colorado, Wyoming, and Texas—and I could go on. Float trips and fishing on Western rivers always seemed to start or end in sagebrush. And I remember an occasional rattlesnake in Texas, Wyoming, Utah, Colorado, and Arizona.

I twisted and stretched a little and could hear the gurgling of a small stream in the gully by the little road. A few bugs were buzzing around—mostly flies, gnats, and an occasional bee or wasp. Things were otherwise quiet except for some cars on the freeway in the distance. Nobody was using the exit I was on.

Looking west by the pungent sage. This is on the westbound side of the freeway and quite some distance from the restrooms.

The little road and pungent sage where the author stopped
to pick up some aluminum cans in 2010. The view is to the
east at the rest stop at milepost 86 on I-70 in Utah.

The eastbound approach to exit 86 on I-70 in Utah.

I had brought two boxes of rocks from an abandoned landscape project that I once started at my home. This was an ideal spot to get rid of them. I tossed out a couple of the larger ones and then lugged the boxes into the brush and dumped them, shaking out all the extra dust. I noticed a number of aluminum cans and decided to pick up a few of them to take home in the empty boxes. Years ago, I was obsessed with collecting cans while helping my son gather over $1,000 worth of them before he finished high school. I suppose it helps the environment to pick up the cans, but I do it for the money. I picked up a dozen cans near my car. This was apparently a good spot for other travelers to stop. Some might toss out a little trash or sneak a "pit" stop. The dry scat near an old cow pie was too big for coyote dung (avid hunters notice stuff like that), but perhaps a cougar. The scat had no hair in it, so I ruled out a cougar. I would think a person would go on to the rest stop that was only a minute or so away. Maybe a big dog while his owner used the site as I did.

I stomped on the cans so they would take up less space. Some of the cans had been in the sun for a long time, and the labels were bleached to where they were hard to read. There were two pint Miller General Draft cans. They were partly flattened, and on the top sides, the print had faded to a shiny aluminum color. The bottom side was still mostly gold in color. I guessed they had been there for at least a year. Some Budweiser cans were all silver on top, but on the bottom, the label still said "one of the world's largest recyclers." My little stop here for "aluminum treasure" was mostly to help me wake up a bit. Years ago, the cans were only worth about half a penny each—but now at 50 cents a pound, my treasure would be almost worth my trouble. Twenty-two cans would be a pound, as I remember from the days collecting with my son. The pint cans were somewhat heavier, I mused, and by now I was sure I already had 50 cents worth. A few cans were under the sagebrush, and as I moved under the branches to reach one, I remembered about rattlesnakes, and I made sure I scuffed the ground and mashed the sage enough to force a snake to announce his presence (if one was there). Now the sage really smelled strong.

One can was partially covered by some camouflage fabric that I tugged on a bit to get the can out from under it. Part of the fabric tore, and I could see that a faded plastic bag inside contained what looked like a rolled-up newspaper. Curiosity made me pull the camo bag out where I could take a look at the paper inside. When I finally wrenched the bag from the sagebrush, I could see that it was a pair of bags like I once used to haul newspapers on the handlebars of my bike. These bags were stuffed as full as possible and were much heavier than any Sunday issue with extra inserts that I had ever delivered. My mind jumped back at least sixty years for that little glimpse into my past. But these papers were in thin plastic tubes to keep them dry in case the lawns had sprinklers on in the early a.m. Three papers came out of one side of the camo bag. The plastic was brittle and faded from some shade of pink. It mostly crumbled away, and the rolled-up newspaper was faded to a pale brown, and it was also brittle. It had been soaked at some time or other and the pages had stuck together, but I could make out that it was a copy of the *Salt Lake Tribune* for Tuesday, April 15, 2008. It must have been there over two years. Most of the print was illegible, but the headlines could be deciphered with a little effort. Apparently, a child had been kidnapped in West Valley City in one story, and another told of three people being hurt in a crash with an SUV and a pickup truck in Bountiful.

I shook three rolled newspapers out of the bag, but the next thing that fell out was a Styrofoam cup with some crumpled brownish newspaper from the want ads. When I took out the wad of newspaper, I found a five-dollar bill and two single dollars with the remains of a rubber band wrapped around them. There were two dimes, a quarter, and seven pennies in the cup. Next, I shook out a brick-sized package wrapped in a stiff gray plastic and tied with some twine. The twine was brittle and broke easily in my fingers. The new twine I use to tie my tomato plants is too tough to break with my hands, so this stuff must have been there long enough to be rotting. The package turned out to be MONEY! The top bill was $20. I was startled beyond description, and I immediately looked around me to see if anyone else was near. I was still alone. Nervously I checked inside the bag again and could see several more brick-sized bundles. I peeked into the other half of the camo bag, and it had no newspapers; but it was bulging full of similar packages of twine-wrapped gray bundles of what I guessed would be more money. I was still alone in that hot, pungent patch of sagebrush, so I quickly dragged the camo bags out and hurried to the car and wrestled them up into the trunk. There was enough money in that first package to make me not want some stranger to find me alone in a very isolated place with a bundle of money.

Quickly, I put my box of aluminum cans in the backseat and put the smaller empty box inside and on top of the cans. I was back on the freeway in only a few seconds and soon was up to highway speed, and I was actually panting with excitement. My heart was pounding. My only guess was that I had found a stash of drug money that had been in the sagebrush long enough to be lost to the people that put it there. It was not a good hiding place. Perhaps the intent was not to hide it so much as to drop it for later pickup by another party. Maybe a ransom payment? Maybe it was marked money, and if I started to spend it, I would be linked to something very sinister. Maybe it was counterfeit. My mind raced to a dozen scenarios. Drowsiness was gone, and I drove on as excited as when I first soloed in an airplane back in my air-force days. In less than an hour, I was at Richfield, Utah.

When I met Arvilla in the parking lot of the Quality Inn in Richfield, I had decided not to tell her about the money. No sense complicating a first contact with a blind date that I found on a singles program on the Internet. She was already checked in on the ground floor of the motel, and she had reserved a room for me on the second floor. We would be spending the next couple of days with some of her family who had come to the little town of Elsinore, where some of them lived. The rest had come to observe "Danish Heritage Day" there. My sociability skills were put to the test as I tried to be good company and not sneak out to the car in the night to see if the stash of money was still there and that the incident was not just some wild dream. Arvilla was nice, and her family was genuinely friendly. We had a good time for two days, but I was impatient to get back to my home in Colorado where I could spread out the money and see how much there was. And also to think about what was going to happen to me with a new female acquaintance.

I got home early Thursday afternoon and took the camo bags into the basement where I could spread the money out on the cement floor where visitors would not come to disturb me and where any stray bugs would be easier to control. There were twenty-two bundles of paper money. The first four bundles in the bag with the rolled papers were $20 bills with two hundred bills per bundle. That would be $4,000. The next bundle was only $1 bills, and again there were two hundred in the bundle. There were nine more bundles in the first half of the camo bags. My heart jumped when the first one of the nine was $100 bills.

"Now we are talking real money," I said to myself. Then . . . "Wow!" I began to shake as I stripped the twine off the other eight bundles, and they were all hundreds! Unbelievable! The jumbled pile of bundles from the second half of the camo bag was also hundreds. I sat on the floor in amazement. At $20,000 per bundle, I was staring at $344,200 and a cup with $7.52 in it. And I can't forget the 50 cents, more or less, in aluminum cans out in the backseat of my car.

The next morning, I took one of the twenties to my bank and asked the teller to check if the bill was possibly counterfeit—because "I had found it in the street." She checked it and even took it to a supervisor and came back to tell me it was okay. Next, I took two of the hundreds to my credit union and deposited them to my account. Nobody called about the bills, and I started making my plans for how I would use up the money without doing any big, stupid things to alert the IRS or the law that I had a bunch of money, which was way out of line with my financial history. There is a problem being an "honest" geologist when the government is involved. Maybe Arvilla will help me spend it. I guess I finally found a treasure—by accident!

EPILOGUE

One of my friends suggested that the title of this book should be *60 Percent Fact and 40 Percent Folly.* The early "treasures" about marbles, golf, topaz crystals, and uranium are as true as I can recall. Even the gold-bearing sample bags of my dissertation were very real, and I was certain I had discovered a new gold deposit. Years later, my students, Dave and Frank, cleverly stumped the old professor when they "salted" my gold pan. Dave still teases me about it. The chicken-bouillon story is as factual regarding the whole mission when we experienced an attack by four B-47 jet bombers on our West Coast cities. It was a test of our defense capabilities on a day when solar flares and sunspots had compromised our radios. We did not know it was a test. A flight engineer did approach me, as a geologist, when I left the cockpit to go aft to supervise the radar technicians. The incident wanders from fact only after I was pulled from my transition flights in the RC-121D to become a weather briefing officer to tell flight crews what weather and surface-water conditions to expect on their flights. I do not know what happened to the two sergeants that were sniping gold from the plunge pool of a waterfall somewhere in California. Instead, I "created" an incident that might have happened to them. A story remotely similar to mine was rumored about in the 1950s. It may have been fiction.

The fishing trip at Lee's Ferry was hatched as I poked around the site and studied the sunken boat under the clear (and very cold) water downstream from Glen Canyon Dam. Because I love the San Juan Mountains of Colorado, it was fun to check that area for Los Tres Cabras mine. That story originally had my two childhood friends in the plot; but when I shared the pilot copies of the text, they asked to be removed from the story because of the unfavorable deception in the story. I don't mind being associated with the story because the whole thing is fiction.

Padre Island was a favorite playground for my family while I worked for Exxon in Corpus Christi, Texas. Hurricane Beulah did little damage to my home in Corpus Christi. But after I moved thirty miles inland to Kingsville, the next hurricane (named Celia) messed up my Corpus Christi home along with fifty-five thousand others in Texas. Luckily, I had sold it. Geologists and weather observers worry a lot about what a hurricane might do to a long, thin barrier island on the Texas coast. Since I was a geologist that had been a weather officer for the USAF, I did spend some time checking out the island after storms. The story about clams on the island is factual until the idea of a shipwreck enters the plot. The professional staff at the National Seashore in 2013 was generous enough to take the photos of the *Donax* clams for me. They need to know that I did not find a wreck, nor did I find anything more exciting than some dead jellyfish that had washed up on the beach with inflated air sacs that would pop under the tires if a car ran over them. You could not miss them all.

Now the Grand Canyon story, about finding some gold in a rockslide in Bright Angel Canyon, is factual until I took the hike from Phantom Ranch to Cottonwood Campground, where I became a crazed nut with serious gold fever and tore up some historic artifacts. When Les Stone found a few flecks of gold in Bright Angel Creek, I imagined all sorts of possibilities. The best one was the rockslide that never happened.

The episode in Westwater Canyon on the Colorado River was all about ants. Panning gold at the Old Miner's Cabin was certainly an interesting part of my little booklet ("Where Is the Gold on the Colorado River"). But as soon as ants enter the story, my gold fever took over again and made a delightful adventure, albeit fantasy, for me. I still wonder if ants can be trained to find gold.

The senorita from Colombia—whom I met on a plane to Los Angeles on my way to a cruise through the Panama Canal—was really a delightful nurse from Grand Junction. We did plan a joke for my dinner group, but when we got to Los Angeles, she went on a cruise to Alaska with a friend. I did get to the emerald outlet and museum at Cartagena, Colombia. My nurse friend did know nurses that worked in Cartagena; but when I think about it, I don't recall bringing home any Hercules Powder boxes full of emeralds. Then there is the incident near the rest stop on I-70 when I was on the way to meet a possible senior companion. I clearly remember kicking around in the pungent sagebrush to ward off rattlesnakes in my search for aluminum cans, but maybe the bag full of other stuff was fantasy. And, oh yes, I married the woman I met. She *is* a treasure!

Index

Edwards Brothers Malloy
Oxnard, CA USA
September 5, 2014